Cover Sculpture © 2012 Vincent De Noux

BACKWASH OF THE MILKY WAY
Science Fiction Adventure Stories

O'NEIL DE NOUX

© 2012 O'Neil De Noux

for STC

1

Author Web Site: http://www.oneildenoux.net
Twitter: ONeilDeNoux

Published by
Big Kiss Productions
New Orleans
First Printing July, 2012

Contents

The Silence of The Sea   Page 5
first published in *Adventure* Anthology, Vol. 1, MonkeyBrian Books,
Nov 2005

Tyrannous and Strong   Page 20
first published in *Asimov's Science Fiction* Magazine, Vol. 24, No. 2,
Feb 2000

A Hot and Copper Sky   Page 43
first published in *Tomorrow Speculative Fiction* Magazine, No. 18,
Nov 1995

Slimy Things Did Crawl With Legs Upon The Slimy Sea   Page 59
first published in *Gorezone* Magazine, Issue 26, Spring 1993

It Rumbled   Page 77
first published in *Oceans of the Mind* Magazine, Issue XIX, Spring
2006, TRIBUTE TO THE GOLDEN AGE ISSUE

Happy Living Things   Page 95
first published in as "Unicorns on Octavion" in *Cricket* Childrens
Magazine, Vol. 33, Nos. 10 and 11, Jun 2006 and Jul 2006 Issues

Upon a Painted Ocean   Page 108
first published in *Fantastic Stories of the Imagination* Magazine, No.
23, Summer 2002 Issue

Things Both Great and Small   Page 124
first published in *Backwash of the Milky Way*

Were Yellow as Gold   Page 131
first published in *Backwash of the Milky Way*

Predator of the Spearmint Forest   Page 145
first published in *Backwash of the Milky Way*

A Frightful Fiend   Page 158
first published in *Backwash of the Milky Way*

Introduction

Along the backwash of the Milky Way Galaxy lies a sun-kissed planet Earthlings call Octavion, a world of sparkling blue oceans, emerald green forests, bright deserts and blue-green lakes. The size of Earth, with a similar star for its sun, Octavion is moonless with an oxygen-rich atmosphere, a planet of colors so vivid they amaze humans. During the day, the Octavion sun raises the temperature into the nineties Fahrenheit. With a nearly non-existent polar tilt, the seasons change so little, they are barely recognized. At night, billowy clouds turn magenta then a deep reddish purple before sinking into a dark indigo before blackness. The stars seem brighter in the moonless sky than on Earth.

The first humans marvel at the beauty of the planet and name its natural wonders for their vivid colors – Cerulean Sea, Cobalt Sea, Sapphire Sea and rivers called Majestic Blue and Royal Blue. The leaves of Magenta Forest are magenta as the bright leaves of the Spearmint Forest reflect that hue. The trees of the Indigo Forest are covered with pale, blue leaves. The stone beneath Lake Violet give its water a purplish cast, limestone of Emerald Lake is green, reflected in his clear water. There is a Copper Plateau and a Terra Cotta Plateau, multi-colored Calico Hills and Cinnamon Hill, the orange-brown color of cinnamon.

Riding the Right of Habitation Act, which gives humans the right to colonize any inhabitable world, people flock to the beautiful planet, only to quickly discover its secret. Octavion is populated by creatures very much like the beasts Earthlings call dinosaurs. Scientist cannot explain this phenomenon. Humans come with their computers and other machines and the inevitable clash of worlds begins, native species edged aside by Earthlings and their farms and ranches, their cows and chickens and horses, cats and dogs. After thirty years, the Indigenous Creature Act is passed to protect native species, giving them the right of way in most instances.

Such is the setting. I hope you enjoy these Science Fiction Adventure Stories.

The Silence of the Sea

Down dropt the breeze,
the sails dropt down,
'Twas sad as sad could be;
And we did speak only to break
The silence of the sea!

"The Rime of the Ancient Mariner"
Samuel Taylor Coleridge (Earth, 1798 a.d.)

For the record, I'm no cartographer. I wouldn't know how to make a map. I just name things.

Watching the sun rise in the western sky above the Perfume Mountains sends a shiver through me. The sky is streaked in pink and bluish purple, indigo high above and shimmering yellow along the mountain tops.

I don my black sunglasses, take another sip of strong coffee and chicory. Rhett snorts as he lies next to my feet, closer to the dying embers of our fire. The right ear of my big, yellow dog rises for a moment, then sinks back like his left ear, which has been floppy since the day I found him rummaging through a garbage can outside my room in that alley back in First Colony City.

Looking up at the mountains again, I yawn. I'd named these mountains two days ago, when I'd discovered them. Called them the Lavender Mountains for their color, until we were close enough to smell the sweet scent in the air. In my journal, I renamed them the Perfume Mountains last night as we set up camp. I reach down and pick up a lavender rock next to my foot and sniff it. Honeysuckle or gardenia, I can't tell which scent, but the very rocks of the Perfume Mountains smell like Earth flowers, clean and sweet.

Rhett lifts his head, looks around and lets out a whine. I pet him.

Rising slowly, Rhett stretches, sniffs the air, still cool from the night and filled with the pungent scent of the perfumed rocks. As I look around, I am again amazed at the colors, the deep lavender of the mountains, the dark green grass of the long plain behind us, the deep blue sky as the sun takes hold of the new day. There are no colors like this on Earth. It's taken years for me to adjust to the depth of the greens and the rich brown hues, the silver deserts and the golden hills of this far away planet we humans have named Octavion.

Twisting the kinks out of my back, I stretch my six foot frame. Still a lean two hundred pounds, even as I approach my fiftieth year (that's Earth years). I run my fingers through my long, unruly hair, as yellow as Rhett's coat. My green eyes are not nearly as dark as the greens here.

I'm Buck. Full name – John Joseph André, namer of names, discoverer of mountain ranges and rivers, plains and seas. I was the first human to gaze upon the vast Silver Desert and the rolling Cinnamon Hills and the Indigo Forest with its dark blue tree bark and pale blue leaves the size of maple leaves. I named each. And now we have the Perfume Mountains. When I return to the Data Registry Center back in that patchwork collection of wooden and stone buildings fancifully called First Colony City, my naming will be official. Here, along the backwash of the Milky Way, we are fortunate to have a couple communication satellites. There are no mapping satellites around Octavion, yet. For now, that's my job.

I don't bother wiping the lavender dust from my hiking boots as I walk over to where my mare and mule graze on the rich grass at the edge of the plain we just crossed. A good seventeen hands tall, Cocoa's coat is chocolate brown except for her white mane and tail. I pat her rump on my way to Charcoal. My mule, coat as dark as sackcloth, doesn't move, except for a twitch of an ear as I dig out a fresh shirt from her pack and an apple. Slicing the apple in half with my Bowie knife I keep sheathed on my left side, I drop half in front of Charcoal's nose. I feed the other half to Cocoa who chomps it with relish.

Rhett finishes off the rest of last night's kill – a plump field hare he caught and we shared, just before sundown. I down the rest of my coffee and make sure our fire's out before putting on my black Stetson.

Saddling up Cocoa, I climb up and announce, "OK. That pass we spotted should be a few miles south of here." I nudge my mare forward and she responds in a nice, even gait, Charcoal following on the long tether.

Moving next to the mountains, I look around for those pterodactyl-like creatures. Last night two of the pesky bastards swooped over us twice before disappearing in the darkness.

"Today is the day I spot a *real* dinosaur."

Rhett, who's inspecting a curious boulder to my left, lopes over in case I'm talking to him. He falls in step next to us.

I'd picked up a rumor in town the night before leaving. A scientist, drinking rum in Margie's Bar, said he was sure there must be tyrannosaurs somewhere along this southern hemisphere. Those fuzzy-headed scientists still have no idea what these creatures are, have no idea how they evolved, why they are so similar to Earth's prehistoric creatures. But this scientist was sure there had to be large predators here.

Reminds me of the environmental scientists still trying to block human colonization of planets because we tend to destroy things. Too bad for them we have the Right of Habitation Act. Humans have the right to colonize any inhabitable planet. Spread our seed to the farthest reaches of the galaxy.

Easing to the left, we skirt the base of a hill toward the opening between two mountains.

"Tyrannosaurs!" I say it aloud as we close in on the pass. That's right, I want to be the first human to see a living tyrannosaur. Narrow and strewn with boulders in various shades of purple, the pass looks perfect for an ambush. If there were any humans within a hundred miles, this is prime bushwhack terrain. I slow down, as we navigate the narrow pass. Rhett darts ahead, sniffing around. As much energy as a puppy, although full grown, he is entertaining.

The pass closes around us and patches of violet trees dot the base of the mountains. I pause for a moment to get a close-up look at the trees whose leaves are thin, like oak leaves. Rhett moves in front and leads us along a narrow gulch for a ways before the sound of running water stops us. Cocoa whinnies.

We follow Rhett through a stand of trees to the edge of a fast-moving creek. The air smells of chlorophyll, only sweeter than the foliage scent back home. Rhett flushes another Octavion hare which scrambles away, escaping into the brambles of burnished-gold bushes with small, teal leaves.

"Come on, boy," I call out and my dog reluctantly follows us through the trees on this bright morning. Again, I am taken by the beauty of this planet, colors that simply dazzle the human eye. A paradise? Maybe. After all, there are no snakes on Octavion.

A mile later, we discover the creek has become a river of sparkling blue water. The color reminds me of the blue on the American flag. We follow it as it rushes between two mountains that seem darker purple than the Perfume Mountains behind us. The violet woods thicken and we slow down. The canopy eventually opens ahead and Rhett barks as soon as we ease onto a wide plateau of rolling copper grass, the river moving to our left, alongside a magnificent blue mountain.

I lean back in the saddle and gaze up at the great blue mountain. Steep and craggy, the mountain is in no way similar to the round-top Perfume Mountains. It is dark blue, bright under the sun. Streaked with the same burnished-gold bushes, it looks like a huge rock of lapis lazuli.

When I was a boy, I visited the Cairo Museum with my father and stood for nearly an hour staring at the funeral mask of the boy pharaoh named Tutankhamen. Solid gold and covered with semi-precious stones, it is still the most beautiful man-made object I have ever seen. Besides the glittering yellow gold, the most striking color was the lapis lazuli adorning the mask.

"Time for preliminary naming," I announce. "The pass we just came through will be Rhett's Pass."

Cocoa snorts as if she understands.

"I know. That's the fourth thing I've named for Rhett."

I pat her mane.

"You'll get your chance. I'm saving your name for something special."

I point to the trees. "The forestry here we'll call the Violet Woods." I wave at the plateau. "This is the Copper Plateau." I point to the blue mountain. "And this is Mount Azure."

What about the river?

I remember the blue color. "It's the American River."

We follow the river for several miles as it seems to wrap around Mount Azure. The Violet Woods enclose us. Just as my stomach grumbles and I'm thinking about lunch, the woods fall away to a continuation of the Copper Plateau. I dismount above a cut back along the river. Rhett races to investigate the river which is over two hundred yards wide now.

I hobble horse and mule on a long tether next to the river. Both drink as Rhett barks wildly at something in the water. Looks like a small fish. I refill my canteens before sitting beneath a violet tree to nibble on jerked beef and the last of the French bread, which is going stale.

It takes a while to realize the dull sound I hear in the background is water. I'd noticed the bend in the river when I refilled the canteens. It runs behind us now, but the sound is different from running water. Can't make it out at this distance.

Rhett comes over for some meat and we eat together. Cocoa and Charcoal munch on the plush grass next to the river. The strong sun is high now. Thankfully the humidity is not. A half hour later, I'm back in the saddle, moving along the riverbank when Rhett stops ahead and stares intently across the river. As we draw close, I hear a low growl come from him.

"What is it, boy?"

As I look across the river, a loud bellow echoes from the woods. A crash precedes a green creature as it rumbles out, heading straight for us. It looks like an armored turtle, about five feet high and maybe fifteen feet long, its back covered with rippled shells. I think they're called anklosaurs. Bouncing as it runs straight for the river, it bellows again.

Cocoa dances in place and I hold her reins tightly. Rhett backs away, barking now. The ankylosaur turns before reaching the river and runs along the far bank. A movement catches my eye at the place in the woods where the ankylosaur came out. A striped beast bolts from the woods. Moving much quicker on two powerful legs, its over-sized head leaning forward, the beast opens its jaws and lets out a shrill roar. About six feet tall, its body has tiger stripes in violet and gold.

Tyrannosaur.

Cocoa rears, almost bucking me off. I struggle to get her under control. Rhett races ahead, paralleling the action across the river. The tyrannosaur doesn't seem to notice us as it bears down on the howling ankylosaur, the sound of fear reverberating in its pitiful howl.

I finally get Cocoa under control and we rush after Rhett.

The tyrannosaur charges the ankylosaur, which swishes its thick tail at the predator. Easily dodging the tail, the tyrannosaur strikes the beast along its left flank. Screeching, the ankylosaur veers toward the river.

Passing through a grove of golden bushes, Cocoa takes the uneven ground well. We catch up to Rhett who pants as he runs next to us now. I have to slow down for Charcoal who brays behind me. Cocoa swerves around a huge bush and turns toward the river.

The tyrannosaur strikes its prey again, slashing at its neck, but the ankylosaur is too heavy and keeps plodding forward. The tyrannosaur falls back and seems content to run behind its prey. They continue at a steady pace. The plateau rises to our right now, then suddenly dips to reveal a small lake ahead. The lake is surrounded by Violet Woods.

Rhett suddenly stops and Cocoa bounces to a stop. Charcoal brays again just as a loud roar echoes from across the river. I pull Cocoa around a large golden bush and watch a thirty foot tyrannosaur race out of the woods close to the lake. It heads straight for the ankylosaur. Darker in color than the small tyrannosaur, which must be a juvenile, the larger predator closes ground quickly. The ankylosaur stumbles.

Another large tyrannosaur comes out of the woods just as the first big one catches the ankylosaur before it can reach the river. Latching to the prey's tail, the tyrannosaur holds firm, stopping the ankylosaur's momentum.

The juvenile tyrannosaur jumps to the other side of the ankylosaur, bites a rear leg. As the second large tyrannosaur arrives, the three predators yank the ankylosaur into pieces, ripping off the entire tail and a leg, leaving the carcass to lie belly up and unmoving.

The juvenile tyrannosaur rips at the exposed flesh where the dead beast's leg was once attached. They eat greedily, ripping the meat, throwing their heads back and swallowing large chunks. They eat quickly.

The woods behind the scene seems to part as an even larger tyrannosaur crashes out. At least forty feet tall, it moves with incredible speed on two thickly-muscled legs. It's got to be a big male. Head lowered, it heads directly for the others. The juvenile sees it first and rips off another chunk of flesh before jumping away quickly.

Closing rapidly, the large tyrannosaur lifts its head and roars so loudly, Rhett jumps behind Cocoa trembles beneath me. The two smaller adults back away, their mouths full of bloody meat. The large tyrannosaur slams its jaws into the belly of the dead ankylosaur. Twisting its head, it places one foot on the carcass and yanks out a mouthful of flesh and bones. It throws back its head and swallows, its snout glistening red with blood.

Cocoa backs away on her own. Rhett notices and runs back the way we came, looking over his shoulder. We pass Charcoal who's snorting as she tries to catch her breath.

I pull on the reins and tell Cocoa, "Slow now, girl."

Over my shoulder, I see the three big tyrannosaurs tearing up more of the ankylosaur, the juvenile darting in to grab another chunk of flesh. As Cocoa leads us away, I watch the large beasts as if mesmerized.

We finally lose sight of them as we move away from the river across the wide plateau, Mount Azure looming on our right now. Taking in a deep breath, the realization of what I've just seen hits me. I'm the first human to see it and the thought sends shivers down my back. I hold the reins tighter to keep my hands from shaking.

I let out a long breath, but still feel the jitters. It was all too fast.

My God. I'm the first human to see tyrannosaurs. Then I chuckle. Others may have seen a tyrannosaur before the great beasts got to them. I'd never seen hunters like these – focused, ferocious, fast.

The sound of water I heard earlier seems louder now as we continue around the mountain. And it occurs to me the river has circled around and is in front of us again, running past Mount Azure. And . . . the sound is too loud.

We continue forward slowly, down a long, gradual incline, following the increasingly louder sound of water. An hour later we come upon the great waterfall and the vast sea beyond. I stop and climb off Cocoa. Rhett moves next to me and we both stand there for long minutes, the roar of the falls nearly deafening, its windblown mist blowing over us – the panorama takes my breath away.

With the great blue mountain behind us, framed by the Perfume Mountains beyond, the river falls into a wide, cobalt blue sea. Even wearing sunglasses, I shield my eyes with my hands as I gaze at the sea. Rhett moves forward, ears lowered, snout sniffing the grass as we walk across the small meadow toward the edge of a bluff. I follow slowly, Charcoal content to nibble grass, Cocoa looking in the direction from which we came. She's still jittery.

Reaching the edge of the bluff, Rhett stops and sits. I reach him a minute later and sit near the edge of the cliff next to my dog on grass cooled by the mist. I gaze out at the wide sea. Below lies is a narrow beach of white sand. The crystal water becomes turquoise with streaks of bright green and purplish blue near the reefs. In the distance, the sea is pale blue, so pale it's hard to tell where the sea ends and the sky begins.

I'll call this the Cobalt Sea. And the small lake where the ankylosaur died, Lake Tyrannous.

Looking back at the huge falls, I know it will be the American Falls for the river that feeds it. A breath of mist flows over my face and I close my eyes and lean back on my elbows. I feel Rhett settle next to me and I lie back, hands behind my head now as I let my steady breathing lull me into a nice nap.

I wake with a start, look back at Cocoa. She's still looking back at the way we came. Charcoal nibbles the grass and Rhett rests at my side. Turning back to the sea I realize what's wrong. I can't hear the sea. The roar of the falls has drowned out the sound of waves rolling to shore. The mist from the falls has blown away the smell of salt water. It's as if I'm looking at a picture of the wide Cobalt Sea.

Glancing at my watch, I'd napped for about a half hour. Rhett lifts his head, grunts and puts it back down as I watch the silent sea. I sit up, lean forward and spot three, large black stains in the water below. Gliding quickly through the clear water close to shore, dorsal fins breaking the water as they rise, then dart deeper. They are Icthyosaurs, hunting beneath the waves, paralleling the beach. I watch them move back and forth three times before rolling into deeper water.

Rhett growls, then barks loudly as two dark green dimetrodons scurry below along the narrow beach. Only about twelve feet long, they are vicious looking. Snapping at one another, their sail fins sway as they dart back into the jungle that runs to the right of the bluff. They slip easily though the tangle of mangrove trees below and disappear in the jungle.

Dark clouds move in from the right, over the sea. The strong Octavion sun is beginning its slow descent, falling toward the sea, streaking the waters with an iridescent glow. Time to start a fire, put up my tent. No sleeping under the stars with those dark clouds hovering offshore.

In a half hour, I have a nice blaze going, Cocoa and Charcoal unpacked and untethered. I open a can of dog food for Rhett and a can of ham for me. As the ham sizzles in its skillet and the beans simmer in their pot, I take my spare canteens to the mist from the waterfalls and prop them up to let the cool river water fill them. Cocoa is still jumpy, raising her head often. I look around too. It's a creepy feeling, as if we're being watched. If it's the Tyrannosaurs, we don't have a chance. I pull out both of my weapons, my .44 caliber Henry Trapper rifle, loaded with seven rounds and my 12 gauge Browning Auto-7 shotgun. Making sure each is loaded, I feel better with these vintage Twentieth Century weapons next to me as I turn over the ham.

Shooting Tyrannosaurs with these weapons will probably only make them angry, but it's still reassuring having them at hand. Rhett finishes his meal and lopes off to where Cocoa and Charcoal are nibbling the lush grass. He doesn't seem to have the same worried feeling, so I feel better. If any of us can sniff out danger, he'll be the first.

I save a slice of ham for Rhett as I eat slowly, washing down the food with the chilled water from the falls. Always nice to have my canteens brimming with crystalline water. The dark clouds are moving away now, content to stay over the sea. A bright orange light illuminates us as the sun hovers above the horizon. A sudden chill along my back causes me to turn in time to see Cocoa running flat out, across the bluff toward the falls. Behind her race two brown predators, smaller than Cocoa, running on two legs.

Raptors.

Snatching up the Henry, I bring it to aim at the raptor closest to Cocoa. Damn, they are so fast, cheetah-fast, moving at incredible speed. I lead it and squeeze off a round, the Henry recoiling against my shoulder. It misses as Cocoa turns our way. The raptors turn and I get a bead on the second one and squeeze the trigger, catching it in the torso. It jumps high in the air and flops to the ground.

I see a flash of yellow as Rhett races for the other raptor, trying to cut it off.

No.

Three Raptors are after my dog, closing in quickly. I level the sights on the one closest to Rhett and drop it. As it tumbles, the other two Raptors jump aside and stop to look at the fallen one. I drop another just as Cocoa's screech turns me back.

The raptor has her by the throat, the claws of its feet slashing at Cocoa's side as the horse continues forward. I grab my shotgun and run for the them. Rhett comes for me, racing hard. Cocoa cries again, a deep painful screech and falls straight down.

I'm still a good twenty yards away, pumping hard. I see jerking movements and it's the raptor, still slicing up my horse. Raising the shotgun, I bear down on them. The raptor raises hits bloody-face and I stop and take most of it off with a clean hit of double-ought buckshot. It rises and twitches and I take the rest of its head off with another shot.

Rhett runs right past me and I turn the shotgun on his two pursuers. I drop the first one ten yards from me and the second turns away, but can't get away. I catch it along its back and send it rolling in a heap.

Turning, I see Rhett heading to cut off two more raptors racing straight for me. I go down on one knee and aim carefully, struggling to control my breathing, and fire at the closest raptor. I clip it and it keeps coming. The second raptor seems surprised at Rhett's speed and raises a claw to strike my dog as it lunges forward. Rhett dodges the claw and strikes the animal high, near the neck and they fall in a rolling heap.

Focusing on the raptor I'd clipped, it's so close, I only have time to point the shotgun and fire. I hit it dead center and the raptor slashes at me as it falls, crashing against my left knee, sending me hard to the ground.

I pick up the shotgun, place it against the raptor's chest and fire again.

That's seven shots.

Reload. I jump up and my left knee gives out. Rising again, I hobble back to my tent. Rhett and the raptor have disentangled and move in a circle, facing each other, Rhett barking, the raptor hissing.

No time to reload.

I drop the shotgun and pull out my Bowie knife.

The raptor sees me, wheels and come for me. I brace myself. The beast accelerates quickly and comes in a gigantic leap, feet first, claws bared. I jump to my right, slashing with my knife, but we both miss. The raptor recovers quickly, turning fast but not in time to fend off Rhett, which catches its throat again and both go down.

I scramble to them and sink my knife in the raptor's flank, all the way to its hilt. Pulling it out with both hands, I plunge it again and again until the beast quits moving. Rising, I stab it one more time, in its throat. Lifting myself from the bloody carcass, I see Rhett lying a few feet away, disemboweled in a large pool of his blood. I crawl to him. Gasping for breath, I feel a well of emotion choking my throat.

Rhett moves. His head turns toward me and I cradle him in my arms. He looks at me, blinks and I can see it there, that familiar loving look my dog has given me again and again.

"I'm here boy." I feel tears in my eyes. "I'm here, Rhett," I tell him as his eyes close and he doesn't move again. Rocking slowly, I hold his head in my arms and let the emotion out.

If there are any more raptors, let them get me.

I don't care.

I can't stop the tears. I don't want to.

• • •

How long I've remained this way, I'm not sure.

A creeping dusk has captured the land.

I gently lay Rhett's head down and limp over to Cocoa. Her eyes are open as she lays there in violent death. Turning, I move back and pick up the shotgun.

Charcoal. I can't see her. Did she run back the way we'd come? Did the raptors get her too? Hobbling to my tent, I pull out my bag of shotgun shells, reload the Browning, tying the bag to my belt. I begin a careful search for my mule.

Certain she's not lying on the bluff, I move to the cliff in case she just ran off. The last flicker of sunlight shades the cliff and but I can't see the beach. Looking back at the dark bluff, I know the only place for me is along the cliff. There I'll have a fighting chance, at close range, with my shotgun.

I inch down the cliff, along a small ledge, barely wide enough for my feet. I follow the ledge down a long ways. Moving around an outcrop, I spot a black blotch in front of me and freeze.

Charcoal brays loudly.

"So there you are, girl." I reach for her, grab her nose and pat it. She nuzzles against my hand and I talk to her in quiet tones, telling her we'll be all right here, praising her for having the intelligence to climb down here where a mule can go and raptors, hopefully, cannot.

I get into a comfortable sitting position, legs dangling off the cliff, shotgun pointing up the slope I'd just descended and wait in the darkness. The moonless Octavion night is too black to see anything. Only the bright stars, reflected on the sea below, reveal we are alive.

Through the long hours, I keep seeing flashbacks of the sudden deaths above and feel a choking sadness. Several times during the night, I sense movement above and brace myself, but nothing comes. The movement returns just before dawn and I watch intently as the first gray light of dawn illuminates the land.

Pterodactyls. Swooping in from the ocean, they flap above us as they land on the bluff. Bastards are eating Rhett and Cocoa. If those hideous-looking vultures are there, no raptors are around. I stand slowly. Surprisingly, my knee isn't that stiff. I climb up as soon as I can see well enough.

The sight on the bluff stops me. It roils with pterodactyls. One peeks its ugly head from inside my tent, many more rise and fall from the sky. I level my shotgun at the nearest and take two out with one shot. The entire colony rises as one, flapping into the sky, swooshing back to the sea.

There is nothing of Rhett left except tufts of fur. I pick up the largest piece, about six inches, and tuck it into my belt on my way

17

to Cocoa. Her skull remains and many of her bones, but that's all. I pick up a loose tooth and pocket it on my way back to my tent.

No fire this morning and no coffee. Wearily, I pack up. I bring my journal to the cliff's edge and sit. I rename the river and the great falls and name the cliff before closing my book.

Shading my eyes, I look out at the blue water of the silent sea.

"I am John Joseph André of planet Earth!" My shout dies immediately in the thunder from the falls. Raising a finger to the waterfalls, I call out.

"That is the Sad American Falls from the river I've named the Sad American River. It's named for the color of the flag of my homeland."

Pointing over my shoulder, I continue, "This is Cocoa's Bluff where my friend died in this place of such beauty." I lower my voice and talk to Rhett. "I guess if you have to die, this is the place, huh boy?"

I tell him something he knows. I tell him how much I'll miss him. Then I tell the ocean, "We have seen what no one has ever seen before, my friends and I. We are the first of our kind here."

Standing, I tell the sea we won't be the last.

"You see, we have come to stay on this planet and there's nothing you can do about it."

It takes me nearly six hours to coax Charcoal back up the cliff, load her down with our supplies and lead her away on foot from the most picturesque place on Octavion. As we start back across the Copper Plateau, I don't look back at the beautiful Cobalt Sea, nor the huge, crystalline waterfalls, nor even up at the magnificence of Mount Azure with its flecks of gold.

At night, when I close my eyes, I try not to remember Rhett snuggling next to me, the softness of his fur when I'd pet him. I've put away the tuft of his coat for now. The memory's too strong now. I'll touch it again, one day, running my fingers through my dog's soft mane.

I dream of Cocoa, racing across the Copper Plateau, long mane flowing in the wind. She's not frightened, not running for her life as she did by the falls. Such a noble beast and look what I brought her to. I don't think of Lake Tyrannous nor the beauty of the Perfume Mountains as we slip through Rhett's Pass back across the long green plain to First Colony City.

• • •

The people at the Data Registry Center look at me with amazement as I log in the names and descriptions of what Rhett and Cocoa and Charcoal and I have discovered. They ask questions, which I don't answer. I tell the frizzy-headed scientist, when he persists on asking more about the Tyrannosaurs, that if he wants more information, go to Lake Tyrannous.

Resupplying takes two days. Finding another horse takes another. Finding a dog takes two more. He's young and eager and blacker than Charcoal with a shiny coat and yellow eyes. I call him Blackie.

My new horse, another mare, isn't as tall as Cocoa, but she's a roam beauty with a feisty disposition. I call her Scarlett. Always loved that book. Charcoal, loaded down with gear, follows us out of town. People have come out to watch us leave. I don't return their waves.

We head in the opposite direction this time. We'll cross the Cinnamon Hills to find what lies beyond. Blackie falls into step next to Scarlett and looks up at me.

I feel a swell in my chest as I realize we're all connected, we'll always be connected. Me and Rhett and Cocoa and Charcoal and Scarlett and Blackie. Earthlings all.

"We're going on an adventure," I tell Blackie. "There are things never seen before and things to name."

Again, for the record, I'm no cartographer. I wouldn't know how to make a map. I just name things.

THE END of "The Silence of the Sea"

Tyrannous and Strong

And now the STORM-BLAST came, and he
Was tyrannous and strong:
He struck with his o'ertaking wings,
And chased us south along.
                    "The Rime of the Ancient Mariner"
                    Samuel Taylor Coleridge (Earth, 1798 a.d.)

Standing on the high cliff overlooking the narrows that separates our island from the mainland, I see an animal that is not supposed to exist in the northern hemisphere of Octavion. I feel my breath slip away as a full-grown tyrannosaur moves out of the Magenta Forest. Its huge head swings from side to side as it steps out on the beach across the narrows. It stops and sniffs the air.

Although I'm wearing sunglasses, I still have to shield my eyes with both hands from the strong Octavion sun shimmering off the brilliant white sand where the tyrannosaur stands. I've never seen one this close before. It has to be fifty feet long and at least twenty feet high.

Green primarily, it's covered with long reddish-brown stripes that remind me of an Earth tiger. The color of its stripes match perfectly the red-brown tree trunks of the Magenta Forest. Its head twists like a bird's head, a huge bird of prey, in jerky movements, as it sniffs the air. It looks up in my direction, and I bend down to hide behind the mangroves that cover the sheer face of this four-hundred foot cliff. I'm downwind, but it keeps sniffing the air. It takes a long look at our island, twists its head again, and scratches the beach with its foot.

It takes three quick steps toward the narrows, pauses, then rushes into the water. It is a dark green-brown stain in the clear turquoise water. Its eyes and nostrils protrude from the water as its long tail propels it, like a crocodile, straight for our island. As it closes in on the small beach below, I peer over the side of the cliff.

It hesitates before coming out of the water, and, for a moment, I hope it'll turn back. But it rises on the rocky beach below like a dragon of death and heads toward the woods to the left of the cliff. It moves stealthily into the extension of the Magenta Forest that covers part of our island.

Doing my best not to panic, I hurry back to my land rover, crank up the engine, and drive back to our stone cabin a good five miles away. My cattle pay the rover no mind as I drive by their pasture. The hogs wallow in their mud pit, oblivious to me as I park the rover between them and the cabin. I look around for a moment, at the peaceful scene, because it'll never be peaceful again. Not with such a beast on the island.

I walk around to the front of the cabin and pause momentarily to look out at the Cerulean Sea to calm myself. Perched atop a low rise, our small cabin overlooks the bright blue sea. The water glistens in the sunlight and looks peaceful. A breeze flows in, as if on cue, and the air smells of salt water.

I pull off my sunglasses and tuck them in my shirt pocket as I step into the cabin.

"Stella," I call out as I move to the gun cabinet.

My computer answers, "Yes, Mac. I see you're back already."

"MacIntyre," I correct her automatically and she ignores my correction, automatically. I reach into the gun cabinet and pull down a Marlin 30-30 and check the lever action. I point it out the front window and dry fire it. The hammer falls smoothly forward with a nice click.

"Stella. Take a priority message."

"Yes, MacIntyre," she answers, a hint of sarcasm in her deep, feminine voice.

I run my hand across the Marlin's black walnut stock and over the blue-steel finish. It feels cool to my touch.

"Yes, MacIntyre. I'm ready." The sarcasm is still there, but she's curious. I like that in a computer.

"A tyrannosaur crossed the narrows this morning and is on the island."

"Unlikely," Stella says. "There are no tyrannosaurs in the northern hemisphere."

"There's at least *one*." I aim the Marlin out the window again, carefully focusing my aim, leveling the hooded brass bead up front between the buck horn rear sight.

"Did you see it yourself?"

"Yes. And I'm going to kill it."

I put the Marlin on the table below the gun cabinet and reach up for the Browning Big Game rifle.

"MacIntyre," Stella's voice is strained. "You cannot kill a tyrannosaur. I suggest we contact the Coast Guard."

At a solid seven pounds-six ounces, the Browning is a beauty, stainless steel with a black oak stock. I pull the lens caps off the Zeiss Supreme scope.

"I'll contact the Coast Guard immediately."

"No," I say. "I repeat, this is a priority message." I let it sink it a second, although I know it only takes milliseconds for Stella to understand. She can be sarcastic, but when I say 'priority', she has to obey. Period.

"All right," she says, icily. "I won't take the time to remind you it is an indigenous creature, therefore you cannot harm it. It has the right of way."

I step over to the open front door and aim the Browning at the lavender tree at the edge of the rise, where the ground falls away to the wide beach below. I'd sighted the new scope only a month ago, calibrating it carefully. I hold it up to my right eye and focus on the tree.

"Please acknowledge," Stella says.

"I have to kill it. I have no choice." I dry fire the Browning.

"The Coast Guard will tranquilize and relocate it."

"The Coast Guard is three hundred miles away."

I put the Browning next to the Marlin and reach into the cabinet for the boxes of bullets, 30-30s for the Marlin, 30-06s for the Browning, all full metal jacket rounds.

"Why don't you just stay in the cabin? Maybe it'll go away."

I open the first box and tell Stella, "Tyrannosaurs don't just go away. There's enough food on this island to feed a herd of tyrannosaurs. Cattle, hogs, iguanodons on the east side of the island and those small ankylosaurs –"

"Nodosaurs," Stella corrects me.

"And one human," I say as I start loading the Browning. "Check your memory. The first settlers. The Sepia Forest. My great uncle was killed by an Octavion tyrannosaur."

"O.K. I'll humor you. How do you propose to kill it?"

"I'm loading my Browning and I'll take the Marlin as back-up."

"Rifles?" Stella's voice rises. "You can't kill a tyrannosaur with a rifle."

"Who says?"

"I'll check my data bank." It takes her two seconds. "There's no record of anyone killing a tyrannosaur with a rifle." She waits for a response.

I finish loading the Browning and start loading the Marlin.

"Maybe you can scare it away."

"Yeah," I answer. "Right."

"It was just a passing thought." She clears her throat. I love it when she does that, since she doesn't have a throat. Then she adds, "Nothing scares a tyrannosaur except a larger tyrannosaur."

"Exactly."

I slip the sixth round in the Marlin, and wish I'd bought one that held more rounds. I pull down my hunting vest and start stuffing bullets in its four pockets, Marlin rounds on the left side, Browning rounds on the right.

"You will not be able to kill it," Stella says matter-of-factly. "It is the largest land predator in the known universe."

"So?"

"You're not listening!"

"I'm listening. I'm just not paying attention." I finish stuffing the vest and start stacking the remaining boxes of bullets in an ammo can.

"I tried calculating the odds," Stella tells me. "But there are no odds. You cannot kill a tyrannosaur by yourself."

I look at the face of her blue screen. "Stella, there isn't *anything* a human can't kill."

She sighs.

I push my point, "If there's one thing history has taught us, it's that a human can kill *any living beast*."

"You are trying my patience," she says.

I snap the lid shut on the ammo can and tell her, as patiently as I can, "Look, its come to eat. Its come to stay. It's a *tyrannosaur*. Its come to rule this island. *My* island. Understand?"

"But you'll get in trouble, even if you do manage to kill it."

"Who's to know?" I walk into the kitchen and start filling plastic water bottles.

It takes her a moment. Her voice is even lower than normal. "Then why did you tell me?"

"So you can tell my sister what happened to me if I don't come back."

She huffs loudly and I have to smile.

"Those weapons are antiques."

She's trying. I don't respond. She knows they are new, even the bullets are less than six months old.

"How long do you calculate it will take you to kill it?"

I pull down my back pack and start shoving jerked beef and vitamins and whatever food is handy inside. Three minutes later, I'm packed and ready. I stack everything in the living room and head for the bathroom.

"How long before I should contact anyone, if you don't return?"

"Don't contact anyone," I tell Stella. "If anyone contacts you after one month, you can tell them. Not before." I go into the bathroom and close the door.

She says something, but I can't hear her in the only room shut off to her.

When I step out, she says, "Please don't do this."

I stop at her monitor and tap it gently with my right hand. "It'll be all right."

"You're patronizing me."

"I know." I turn back to the gun cabinet and pull down my flare gun. Then I stuff it and as many flares as I can into the back pack.

"As soon as you leave, I'm calling the Coast Guard."

"No you're not. This is a priority message. You *cannot*. You're incapable." I look around in case I've forgotten anything.

"I'll find a way. If there's one thing history has taught us, it's that a computer can outmaneuver a human. Given the time."

"Take your best shot, darling." I scoop up the Browning and the back pack and walk out. It takes me three trips to move everything into the rover.

Stella has the last word on my final trip out. She says, "I'm working feverishly to override your command. I predict success imminently."

"I love you too," I tell her as I leave.

Before driving off, I walk to the other side of the cabin and brush the leaves off my wife's tombstone. I kneel next to it and pick a leaf off my daughter's smaller tombstone.

"Well, Sweetheart," I tell my wife. "I might be seeing you two very soon. A tyrannosaur just crossed the narrows."

I close my eyes and see her face again, her lapis-blue eyes, her warm smile, her long red hair flowing in a breeze from the Cerulean Sea. It's hard envisioning my daughter's infant face, except that it is tiny and round and as beautiful as an angel.

I can almost hear my wife's voice answer me.

"A tyrannosaur? On *our* island?"

How she loved this place. Wouldn't leave it, not even for childbirth, not even when the fever struck three months later and she and our daughter faded. She knew I'd called the Coast Guard, for all the good it did. By the time they arrived, she and our baby were gone.

I look back at the cabin we built, then up at the cobalt blue Octavion sky.

This beautiful, unforgiving world, this mystery of the galaxy, drew our grandparents, like thousands of other earthlings. Just as this island drew my wife and I.

While scientists, like my father, racked their brains, trying to discover why Octavion's dinosaurs are so similar to earth's prehistoric beasts, we built a life. The scientists are no closer to solving this great riddle of the galaxy.

I know better than to ponder these things. *Why* isn't important to me. *Why* a tyrannosaur exists on the northern hemisphere isn't important. It's *here*. And I have to do something about it.

My knees crack when I stand up. "Forty and I'm falling apart," I tell my wife. I see her face again. In my mind, she's eternally young at thirty. Dead five years now, it seems longer. I stretch, then tell her, "Either I'll kill it or it'll kill me."

A breeze blows across me and I smell the sea again. I pull my sunglasses out of my pocket and put them on as I walk back to the rover. I hesitate, then go back into the cabin, pulling off my sunglasses as I sit in the lounge chair and ask Stella, "Please give me all the information you have on tyrannosaurs."

"I'm glad you came back. You must reconsider your decision. I've calculated the odds and–"

"Stella. Give me whatever information you have on tyrannosaurs."

She sighs and then says, "My information is limited. I'll access the central library in Scarlet City."

"No," my voice raises. "Nice try."

I have to ask again before she spouts out, "The tyrannosaur of the planet Octavion is fifty feet long, twenty feet high and weighs four tons. Its head is five feet in length. Its teeth are up to seven inches long and serrated, like a butcher's heavy chopping knife. It is warm blooded and tenacious in its pursuit of prey. It can run as fast as forty miles per hour. It is a most adept hunter and also a scavenger, robbing lesser predators of their prey.

"That's all I have in my data bank. May I please access the central library –"

"No," I cut her off, rise and put my sunglasses back on. "See ya'," I say as I leave.

"The odds are against you. Approximately one thousand, one hundred and fifty to one."

I walk out on the porch. Behind me she says, "I'm still attempting to override your command, Mac. I predict success."

I walk back in, reach down and unplug the telephone line.

"Override this," I tell her.

"What did you do?"

"Ciao, darling," I tell her on my way out again.

"Mac! MacIntyre! What did you *do*?"

On my way back to the rover again, something Stella said gives me an idea. She called it a scavenger. I go into my shed and scoop up a canvass tarpaulin, open the back of the rover and lay the tarp inside, leaving the rear door open. I back the rover up to my smoke house. I grab a pair of gloves, a meat hook, and the stainless steel cart, and wheel out a side of beef to lay on the tarp in the back of the rover.

The smoky scent of cooked beef fills the rover as I crank up the engine. My empty stomach rumbles. One of my cows looks up at me as I leave her and the others in their ignorant bliss and drive back toward the cliff.

I keep a sharp look out as I drive to a wide meadow, which is the only way up from the cliff, through the forest. The meadow is about a mile across, with woods on three sides, woods that fall away to cliffs. The woods to my right and in front are the extension of the Magenta Forest, thick tree trunks and green foliage. The woods to my left are mostly mangroves and puzzle trees, too thick for a tyrannosaur to navigate.

I pull the rover off the dirt road and drive to the center of the meadow to a small rise. The ride is bumpy and I have to slow down. The dark green grass looks nearly black in places. I stop the rover and climb out. The grass is up to my knees. I pull out the side of beef and drag it up on the rise where the grass is shorter. I pull out my Bowie knife and slice off two thick strips of beef, which I bring back to the rover.

I drive back to the road and set up a good firing position. The forest to my right is too close, less than a hundred yards away, so I point the rover back the way I came, the forest on my left now. I move over into the passenger seat, the Browning pointing out the open window.

I scope out the rise and can see the side of beef clearly in my sights. Sitting back, I grab my binoculars in one hand and use the Bowie knife to cut off slices of beef with the other. The meat is juicy and delicious and surprisingly tender. I make note to cut down the smoke house time in the future. If I have a future.

I wash down the beef with cool water and empty an entire water bottle finishing off the tasty beef. I keep scanning the meadow and the forest around me as I wait, as the sun creeps high in the sky. At least a Cerulean breeze continues flowing over our island, cooling me in the mid-day heat. I take off my vest and drape it over the back of the seat. My sweat-covered khaki shirt, pressed against me, cools me with each breath of sea breeze.

Slowly, I scan the forest around the meadow and even watch the mangrove woods for the beast. I wish I'd brought coffee. An hour slips by, then another. And I wonder if the damn thing has already moved past me and is now feasting on raw beef back at my cabin.

I readjust myself in the seat and keep scanning the forest. My eyes are getting tired, but I keep looking as another hour passes. Then, I see it. The beast steps out of the forest at the far edge of the meadow. I blink, rub the sweat from my eyes and look back through the binoculars. I was looking right there and hadn't seen it, its camouflage is so perfect in the woods.

Raising its head, the tyrannosaur sniffs the air, and looks around. It takes a hesitant step forward, lowers its head, and rushes for the side of beef. I grab the Browning and push my right eye against the sight. The tyrannosaur is so fast, it's at the beef before I can get into a comfortable firing position.

It hits the beef at full speed, raising it high, snapping its head to slice the side of beef in half. The tarp flies into the air. The tyrannosaur throws its head back and swallows the beef. I aim carefully and start squeezing the trigger.

The tyrannosaur lowers its head and I set my aim square on its forehead. I squeeze slowly, keeping the cross-hairs in place until the Browning kicks against my shoulder and I see it strike the great beast in the forehead. The loud report echoes across the meadow. The tyrannosaur flinches, then lowers its head again and steps back to gobble up the rest of the beef. I aim again, this time just below its left eye, and fire. Its head snaps back slightly.

I smell my sweat along with the acidic smell of gunpowder from the bullets. I aim again. The tyrannosaur's mouth opens and it bends its head back and roars. I aim at its throat and shoot again. I see it hit the neck and see the tyrannosaur react, snapping at the air now. I aim again and it bolts, racing back for the forest. I squeeze off a fourth shot but miss.

It's too fast. I fire a fifth shot, but it isn't even close. Two heartbeats later, the tyrannosaur disappears into the forest not far from where it had come out.

Damn! Damn! Now I have a *wounded* predator on my hands.

Maybe my shots will take it down eventually. *Yeah. Right!*

I pull the Browning back in and grab the Marlin as I slip over into the driver's seat. I raise the binoculars but cannot spot the beast. I keep looking for any movement in the forest. I wait. Then, I pull the binoculars down as I feel a shudder. Is it the ground? Or am I shaking so hard? Or is it my thundering heart?

I feel pin pricks along my neck.

I look at the forest closest to me. Nothing.

I wait.

Then I put the binoculars down and wipe my eyes. What the hell am I waiting for? A voice in my mind that says, "Get out. Get out now!"

I start the engine and look around, and it comes out of the forest not a hundred yards away, rushing right for me. The ground shudders. The rover kicks over and I slam it into drive and hit the gas. The rover flies down the dirt road, kicking dust up behind me, and I see the tyrannosaur angling to cut me off. It's so big and so *fast*. I push the accelerator and quickly realize it has the angle on me.

What the hell was I thinking? I was going to kill *that* with a rifle?

The bastard is smart enough to cut me off, angling for the road ahead of me. I have to go cross-country. I slam the brakes and skid to a grinding stop, shift into four-wheel drive and punch the accelerator, taking a hard right turn into the meadow.

The rover bounces and I have to slow down. I'm doing less than forty now, and its gaining on me, so I accelerate and bound up and down across the meadow. The Browning flies out the passenger window, the Marlin smacks me on the arm and falls to the floorboard. Water bottles boomerang around the cab. My vest rises then falls as I bounce off the seat and hit my head on the roof.

The beast roars and I feel my stomach jump. It's closer now, running hard, right for me. I shove down the accelerator and the rover lurches and gains ground. I see woods in front of me and race for it – mangroves and thick-branched puzzle trees. Maybe the ground is smoother near the woods. Maybe I can skirt the woods and get back to my cabin and hide and call the Coast Guard and pray.

Then, in a heart-sinking moment, I'm airborne, springing high and coming down hard. The rover bounces twice, bottoms out, hits something, and I'm airborne again, twisting in mid-air. The rover slams sideways to the ground and flips over and over. I hold on to the steering wheel as I hit the roof and then the seat then the roof again. Until, with a hissing and groaning, the rover slides to a stop. I'm upside down, the roof partially crushed. The engine whines, then coughs and dies. Smoke and dust choke me and I pray it's not on fire.

I reach to unbuckle my seatbelt, but it's jammed. As I wiggle, my left knee stings in pain. I look down and it's twisted in an awkward position. I catch my breath, pull out my Bowie knife and cut away the seat belt. I slide to my right and pain shoots up my knee as I straighten my leg.

My elbows are scraped and bloody and I wipe my face with my hands, glad to see it's sweat and not blood. My left leg throbs as I look around. And the ground shudders. I watch the tyrannosaur arrive. It slows, but doesn't stop completely, circling the rover. Then a deafening roar reverberates though the rover, causing my teeth to chatter.

It raises a foot and kicks the rover, shoving it a good ten feet. Grass clumps up on my right. The huge, three-toed foot raises again and kicks the rover, spinning it completely around. A sharp explosion above is followed by a hiss.

It bit a tire. Then it bites another.

I keep still as I hear it sniffing above and then around the sides of the rover. I sees its snout now, probing, bumping against the side of the rover. I smell blood and see a trace of red on its snout. It growls and sniffs again.

The head rises and I watch its feet. It circles the rover again. Then, it backs away and waits. A loud roar makes me jump and I close my eyes. It roars again, higher-pitched, and then moves a little further away.

I watch it move away slowly, sniffing the ground as it goes. It turns back three times, but keeps moving away until it reaches the forest. Turning once again, it looks at the rover and roars, then slips between the red-brown trees and green foliage and disappears. I look out at the mangroves not fifty yards from where I lie. Carefully, I pull myself forward and manage to squeeze to the open passenger-side window. I grab the back pack, but it's stuck. My knee aches as I yank on the pack, and it rips as it comes out. I hold on to the bottom and try to find the Marlin.

I keep watching the Magenta Forest, in case the beast comes out again.

Sweat fills my eyes and I wipe them again.

Sliding out of the rover to the black-green grass, I look again for the Marlin, but can't find the damn thing. The pin pricks are back along my neck and I turn to the mangroves and crawl away as fast as I can, my knee throbbing with each movement. At least I can move it, even bend it, so it's not broken.

Wrenched, I tell myself as I get close to the mangroves. It's dark in there, and I rise and limp into the safety of the darkness. As I reach the first puzzle tree, I lean against it. Surprisingly, I can put some weight on my knee.

I hear a noise, a distant roar. No, it's more like a scream. I move into the mangroves, climbing over twisted branches, squeezing between the large tree trunks. I keep looking back at the bright meadow and find a nice branch to sit on to rest a moment. Then I see the tyrannosaur, standing across the meadow at the edge of the Magenta Forest. I see a movement to its right. It's a nodosaur. I realize I still have the binoculars around my neck, so I lift them and watch.

The nodosaur is only twenty, maybe thirty feet from the tyrannosaur. It's looking at the huge beast and backing away slowly. The tyrannosaur looks around and then lowers its head, snaps and rushes the nodosaur. Although the nodosaur is nearly twenty feet long, with oval-shaped plates and spines on his back and sides, it's no protection against the tyrannosaur. The big beast rams the nodosaur with its head, and the nodosaur rolls. The tyrannosaur is so quick; it pins the nodosaur down with one foot and bites a huge chunk from its throat. I see blood gush and pull the binoculars away.

Then, as if I'm hypnotized, I put the binoculars back up to my eyes and watch the great predator feast. Its blood-slick snout rises from the nodosaur. Its jaws open and bite down, head twisting as it yanks away another large chunk of meat. Then I see something unexpected. The huge jaws seem to expand, to open sideways so it can swallow more easily.

Lord.

I get up and move through the mangroves and puzzle trees, trying to work my way through them toward my cabin. I don't get twenty yards before I have to stop. The branches are too tangled, I can't squeeze through. So I work my way back, put the back pack on the same branch I sat on earlier and pull out a water bottle.

No longer cool, the water still tastes sweet, I drink too much and have to force myself to stop. I search the back pack and see the

32

flare gun is still there, but only two flares are left inside. I pull out a piece of beef jerky, but put it back.

Lifting the binoculars, I see the tyrannosaur is no longer across the meadow. Whatever's left of the nodosaur is hard to distinguish at this distance. OK, I tell myself, what do I do now? Should I try to slink home after dark? What if the tyrannosaur is a better hunter at night? What the hell do I do now?

I wipe sweat from my eyes again and see my wife's face for a moment. So I close my eyes and snap-shots appear in my mind, pictures of us discovering our island, of our first nights in the tent we'd brought, of the long seasons building our cabin and our ranch, of the years spent toiling beneath the relentless Octavion sun, making something of our island. Opening my eyes, I gaze at the meadow, and, as if in a heat-driven daze, I see the empty years I've spent alone, keeping what was left of our island together, going through the motions, toiling to keep it. And now, maybe, I'm near the end.

As if to answer me, the tyrannosaur comes racing out of the Magenta Forest again and runs headlong across the meadow, straight for my rover. Barely slowing, it rams the rover and sends it sailing. As soon as the rover hits the ground, the tyrannosaur is on it again, biting off part of the roof and a door, flinging the pieces aside.

Then it stops, backs away, and takes a careful look at the rover. Craning its head down, it sniffs it and starts moving around the rover, sniffing the ground. It moves back to where the rover rested before its last attack and nuzzles its snout to the ground. And, slowly, it moves toward me.

Like a bloodhound, it hones in on me, heads straight for me, and stops just outside the tangle of mangroves. I sink down behind the puzzle branch and peek out at the beast. I hear its sharp, snorting breaths. Its deep-set orange eyes peer right at me, and blink. This close, I see its eyes face forward, like a human's, like a predator's.

It growls a low, deep growl, opens its jaws slowly, and roars at me. I fall back from the impact. It is a terrifying sound, a rumbling deep from within the great beast that makes me shiver. It gives me the shakes yet I stare back at the cold eyes. It moves forward and bites at the mangroves, ripping the trees, tearing away the twisted branches. Tossing them aside with a jerk of its huge head, its jaws snap down on more trees as it works it way toward me.

Go eat something else, you moron. Something bigger. There's cattle on the other side of the island.

I back away through the mangroves, climbing over gnarled branches. My knee aches in response. The beast keeps coming, its dagger teeth slashing the foliage, snapping the trees. I worm my way around a large tree as the tyrannosaur rips up two mangrove trees at once, then spits them out.

It's no moron. It has to kill me. I *hurt* it.

Looking around, I see two huge puzzle trees close together, mangroves wrapped around them and I crawl between them. A minute later I can go no further. I look down, but cannot even reach the ground.

Its right behind me now, bending its head forward, sniffing me out.

It sees me and presses its snout between the huge tree trunks. It can't reach me. It backs up a step, snarls, then presses its snout between the trees again. Its jaws open, and the smell of dead flesh washes over me. I see bloody meat caught between its dagger teeth.

Then, like a tremendous snake, the tyrannosaur's black tongue slithers out and reaches for me. It's forked and moves around slowly from left to right, probing between the mangrove branches for me.

Pushing as far back as I can, I pull out my bowie knife and hold it high. The tongue flicks my way and I slash it, drawing a red slice of blood. The beast pulls back and roars in defiance. It looks at me, switching eyes as it peeks in.

Throwing back its head it roars louder than ever, then begins tearing at the puzzle trees with its feet, kicking and slashing with the three large talons on each foot. Splinters fall against me and I press back away from it.

The tree on my left begins to lean away as the tyrannosaur bites at it like a mad dog, growling as it bites. It's so large and so close now, I smell its musty flesh and feel myself gagging. I raise the Bowie knife high. Three mores bites and the puzzle tree is splintered.

The tyrannosaur opens its jaws and shoves its ugly mouth at me. I'm shaking so hard, I have to hold the knife with both hands and slash at the mouth, slicing its lower lip. The tyrannosaur bellows and pulls back.

Then it slams its face into the opening it made between the trees and bites at me. I pull back and it still can't get me. It keeps trying, teeth snapping, and I feel a sudden sting on my right arm.

I hear myself scream as I plunge the Bowie knife into the beast's lower lip. It jerks back and the knife falls out of my hand. The tyrannosaur takes a step back and snaps its jaws at me. I look down and see the knife sticking up in ground next to my left leg. I reach for it, but can't get to it.

The tyrannosaur lunges forward, its jaws snapping inches from my head. I reach down as far as I can until my fingers touch the knife's handle. I can't get a grip, but I can push the knife against my leg, then lift my leg slowly until I grab the Bowie, the deadly jaws snapping inches from my face. I slash out again at the beast's mouth. It backs away again.

Frantically, I wipe the sweat from my eyes and see that my right arm is bleeding and realize one of the seven-inch dagger teeth has nicked me. The tyrannosaur continues backing away, still watching me. I wait one heartbeat, then another, then another. Holding my knife high, I reach into the back pack and find the flare gun.

The tyrannosaur cranes its head to the side as it watches me.

I fumble with the flare gun, crack it open, and shove a flare inside. I barely have time to close it, as the tyrannosaur comes for me again, jaws open.

I point the gun into the beast's mouth, but wait until it's only a few feet away before firing. The flare disappears inside the mouth. The monster hesitates. I smell sulfur and the tyrannosaur jerks its head back, then jumps away from me, throws its head back, and roars a high-pitched roar. It jumps back again and leans its head forward and coughs, and the flare bounces out.

Simmering, the flare ignites with the fresh air and the tyrannosaur jumps away from it.

Move. I have to move.

I push my way out and stumble, as fast as I can through the mangroves to my left. I plunge headlong, fighting my way through the branches. I know it's behind me. I know it won't stop. I go down on all fours to squeeze under some branches and look back.

The tyrannosaur is kicking at the flare now. Dirt flies as it kicks. The bastard's putting out the flare.

I find I can move between the mangroves if I keep moving to my left, paralleling the meadow. Knowing the flare won't occupy it long, I move as fast as I can. Tripping, I fall behind a puzzle tree and stop to catch my breath.

I use the Bowie knife to slice off a piece of my shirt to wrap around the cut on my right arm. It isn't as bad as I thought, more of a scrape than a cut, but I know the scent of blood will only help the tyrannosaur. I hurry forward and see the meadow more clearly now. Using every ounce of strength, I press forward, bolting and lunging, jumping and crawling.

I know its back there. I know it'll come for me. It'll never stop.

Then I hit an open area as the mangroves fall away and the puzzle trees are replaced with the towering red-brown trees of the Magenta Forest. I stop and look at the meadow. I'm only fifty yards from it now, and know a low cliff lies to my left and the cliff where I first saw the tyrannosaur is about two hundred yards across the edge of the meadow.

If I stay here, it'll have no problem hunting me down in the forest.

If I can make it to the high cliff, I might be able to work my way down into the mangroves and hide along the sheer face of the cliff. I see myself clinging to the mangroves, like a monkey, while it can't reach me from above or below.

Then I hear it behind me, snorting and sniffing.

I go down on my haunches, my knee on fire, and see it as it moves along the meadow, tracking me. I go back into the mangroves and fight my way to the low cliff that falls away gently to the savanna along the east end of my island.

The tyrannosaur moves into the Magenta Forest and follows me.

I can move through the mangroves quicker. But I'm so tired now, I ache everywhere.

Moving around a scruff pile of dead mangroves, I slip and fall, and feel wetness. It's water. I'm sitting in a cool stream I didn't know existed. I lean forward and shove my face into the bubbling water and its so good it sends a shiver through me. I drink and drink and only lift my head to catch a breath before drinking more.

Pulling my head out, I listen for the beast, but hear nothing.

I dare to peer around the scruff pile and there it is, moving slowly into the mangroves from the forest. I reach into the back pack, pull out the flare gun, load it, and fire the last flare into the scruff pile. Then I back away, as, with a sudden popping, the dead wood ignites in a wall of flames between me and the tyrannosaur.

If it gets through that, it can eat me. I give up.

I watch the flames rise as I lean back against a low mangrove branch. The tyrannosaur bellows, but the fire roars back and rises high into the trees and pushes out on both sides now. The wind guides the fire toward me and the low cliff.

If I push hard, I might be able to skirt it and slip back into the Magenta Forest behind the beast. I look back, and my God, the beast is trying to get through the fire, snarling at it, kicking at the burning mangroves. I keep going and lose the tyrannosaur in the smoke.

Reaching the edge of the forest, I look around, but can't see it. If it's lurking in the woods, I'm dead. If it moved out into the meadow to get at me that way, I have a chance. Catching my breath, I take a careful look around.

Then I bolt, hobbled by my limp, and race headlong through the forest. I make good time, my heart stammering, my body aching with each step. Then I hear it and stop, lean against a tree, it roars again.

And thank God. Its on the other side of the fire, in the mangroves, searching for me.

I keep going, keep running, keep moving on and on, and the roar of the fire dies away behind me. When I finally reach the edge of the forest, I stop to catch my breath. The sheer cliff where I first saw the beast is only twenty yards in front of me, the meadow to my right now.

Slower now, I cross over to the mangroves at the top of the cliff and look down at the turquoise water. My hands raise to shielding my eyes and I spy a dark object moving in the narrows. It comes up and a spout of water rises as an ichthyosaur belches out air.

"Where the hell were *you* when the bastard swam over?"

I take in a deep breath and check myself. My arm has stopped bleeding. I remember dropping the back pack earlier, but my binoculars are also gone, and my jaw hurts.

A cool, sea breeze wafts up at me and I feel a sudden chill. Goosebumps dot my arms. I turn slowly and it's there, not a hundred yards away, standing in the meadow, looking at me. It twists its head to the side, bird-like, lowers its huge head, and rushes for me.

I scurry into the mangroves and start climbing down the cliff. The green mangrove vines are not as thick nor as strong as the wooded mangroves above. I sway as I descend and bump back into the cliff just as the tyrannosaur arrives above, sending a cloud of dirt down on me. It roars at me.

I duck, then climb further down, the vines not as sturdy here. I hold on and look up. The tyrannosaur leans down and snaps its jaws at me. More dirt tumbles down. I close my eyes. When I open them, I'm startled to see the great beast is leaning further down. Its right foot anchored in the mangrove trees at the cliff's top, its small hands gripping the mangroves along the cliff's face as it leans down to get at me.

The mangroves shudder, then shake, and I fall a few feet, but the vines hold.

It roars at me and belches its acidic, dead-meat breath at me. It snarls and snaps and grinds its teeth, its orange eyes glistening at me. I try to move to my side, but the mangrove vines are thinner there.

Then the vines shake again and I skid down several feet, my arms scraping against the side of the cliff. Dirt and rocks rain down on me and I shut my eyes again. When the turbulence stops, I look up, and the great beast is silent.

It looks funny, and I realize it's leaning back against the cliff top, using its great weight to keep from pulling down the vines. It growls at me, its eyes watching me. I hear another noise, a strange, yawning sound. It is the sound a tree makes when its trunk is slowly breaking.

The mangroves.

They're giving way.

I look up and see some of the roots coming out above me and next to the tyrannosaur. I hold on. It is then I realize the beast is holding on too. Its only movement is the rise of its chest with each deep breath and the movement of its deadly eyes as it watches me.

Slowly, cautiously, I pull myself up just out of the great beast's reach. It growls at me. I keep going. Although I'm exhausted, I find the strength to pull myself up. I have to stop after each movement. But I manage to move up even with the beast along the cliff, and it snarls and snaps its jaws at me.

Wrapping vines around both legs, I pull out my Bowie knife and start cutting away the mangroves. Every few seconds, I look at the orange eyes and they leer back at me, mean with hate. And slowly, inexorably, the vines snap and the tyrannosaur begins to dangle. It squirms once and pulls more vines free and stops, its front claws digging into the side of the cliff to keep from falling.

As soon as the mangroves quit moving, I untangle my legs and scramble up to the top of the cliff. I race around the tyrannosaur and start hacking away at the mangroves where its right foot is anchored. It roars back in defiance and whips its huge tail at me. I duck under it and lie down on my stomach.

Using both hands, I chop at the branches, cutting through one, then another, suddenly, with a loud snap and a sudden rush the mangroves give way and the tyrannosaur falls free four-hundred feet down to the rocky beach below.

It bounces and falls heavily into the shallow water along the beach, and does not move.

"Ha!" I hear myself yell down to the beast. "It's called gravity, ass-hole!"

And I start laughing as I lie there, my arms so weak I can barely move them, my knee numb with pain, my body so battered I ache over every inch. And I keep laughing, until I feel lightheaded. I close my eyes and wait for whatever strength is left in me to return. Later, I sit up, on the cliff's edge, and look down at the tyrannosaur.

Its neck is twisted, its body contorted in a pretzel position. And a bright red stain surrounds the great beast. Shielding my eyes again with my hands, I watch the strain grow. Some time later, I spot the first ichthyosaur cruise past. It turns and cruises by again.

A few minutes later, the first ickys strike the tyrannosaur. I watch as they dart in, tear off a piece of the great beast, and swim away at great speed. And ever so slowly, the ickys drag the body from the shallows, devouring it in pieces, reddening the bright turquoise water.

I watch until the early evening rain comes, like clockwork, and washes across our isle from the Cerulean Sea. I smell the smoke behind me as the long rain puts out the fire I started. Opening my mouth, I lean back and drink the rain and it's so good.

It takes a while, but I manage to stand up, slip the Bowie knife back in its sheath, turn my back to the narrows, and limp away through the meadow. Finally, I reach the dirt road where I'd positioned the land rover to take pot shots at the tyrannosaur that morning, a lifetime ago. I move down the road slowly, thankful for each painful step. The rain eventually stops, as suddenly as it started, and the sky is streaked in purple and blue and orange.

It's almost dark by the time I reach home. The Octavion sun is blood-red as it falls beyond the far horizon, like a red disk sinking into the Cerulean Sea. I stand outside our cabin for a moment and watch the sunset. Rust-red light cloaks the land. The red light follows me into the cabin, giving the front room a crimson glow, casting my shadow like a black ghost across the furniture.

"Mac?" Stella calls out. "Mac, is that you?"

I realize I'm grunting as I walk. As I pass, I tell Stella, "MacIntyre."

"Oh, MacIntyre! Are you all right?"

"I'll tell you in a minute."

I move into the hall.

"What?"

"I have to go to the bathroom."

"Oh."

I draw a sink full of water, shove my face into it, then wipe away the grime with a towel. Looking up in the mirror, I see a pair of bloodshot green eyes looking back. My face is nicked with cuts and my jaw is bruised. My hair, has been more gray than brown for a while now, looks as if I just stepped in from a windstorm. I almost laugh at the comical face in the mirror.

I go back out into the kitchen and grab a chilled water bottle from the refrigerator before plopping on my sofa. I take a long, cold drink of water, my throat tightening with the sudden coolness.

"Well," Stella says. "What happened?"

"I need a new land rover."

Four seconds later, Stella's voice drops an octave, "MacIntyre! What happened?"

"I'm all right. A little banged up, but I'm O.K."

"What about the tyrannosaur?"

"Dead." I take another drink.

Stella pauses, probably for effect, before she says, "Well, you were right. There isn't anything a human can't kill."

Suddenly, I feel nauseous. Sitting up, I put the water bottle on the end table, close my eyes and rub them. I see stars momentarily, then see the great beast lying in the shallows, the red stain

41

expanding around it and I feel sad, very sad, as if I'd done something terribly wrong.

"I had no choice." I say it aloud before realizing.

"Of course you didn't," Stella agrees. Then she clears her throat and says, "That wasn't funny. Disconnecting the phone line."

I almost smile. "Actually. It was funny."

Pulling my legs up on the sofa, every muscle aching, I lie back and close my eyes.

"If you reconnect the phone line, I can summon medical help." Stella won't give up.

"Stella. This is a priority message. Erase all reference to this tyrannosaur from your memory."

"Of course. But when you've rested, you have to tell me everything." She pauses, the adds, "You really killed it. I'm so proud of you."

I want to tell her I didn't kill it. Gravity did. But what's the use. The last thing I am is *proud.*

I smell the sea again as a breeze floats in through the open front door. I'm not getting up to close it. My steady breathing soon causes me to drift and I feel sleep coming on.

Again, I say it aloud before realizing. "I had no choice."

"Of course," Stella agrees. "It was either you or it. You had no choice."

"Don't patronize me."

"I'm not. You had no choice."

If I keep telling myself that, maybe I'll believe it one day.

A moment later Stella tells me, "You'd better get some rest."

"Yes, mother."

"That's not funny!"

THE END of "Tyrannous and Strong"
for my son Vincent

A Hot and Copper Sky

All in a hot and copper sky,
The bloody Sun, at noon,
Right up above the mast did stand,
No bigger than the Moon.

"The Rime of the Ancient Mariner"
Samuel Taylor Coleridge (Earth, 1798 a.d.)

She lived in a cabin on a bluff overlooking the Cobalt Sea on planet Octavion. Sometimes, when the wind blew in from the east, she would stand outside her cabin to feel the windblown mist from the giant waterfalls of the Sad American River as it plummeted down Mount Azure into the sea. Afternoons, when the sun's harsh rays were strongest and even the pterodactyls refused to take to the sky, she would cross the meadow behind her cabin to the edge of the falls and cool herself in the swirling vapors of the sparkling river water. Later, she would lay on the flat boulders near the base of Mount Azure and gaze up at the magnificence of the Perfume Mountains.

Her name was Daryn, and this afternoon she strolled naked across the meadow, a towel draped over her shoulder. A tall woman, nearly six feet, Daryn's long brown hair reached half-way down the back of her lean, svelte body. She had striking features, a sharp nose and a pointy chin, softened by full lips and large green eyes. Her breasts, matured by her thirty years, were a hint oversized with small, round nipples. In the strong sunlight, the red highlights of her hair stood out.

Nearing the falls, Daryn placed her towel on a small bounder and walked into the mist. The roar of the water was nearly deafening, but she felt no particular danger so close to the huge falls. She remained a good hundred meters from the edge of the cliff, turning slowly, as the cool water bathed every pour of her body. She pulled her hair back and then ran her hands down her sides.

43

She felt a rush of excitement as she turned in the mist. She felt someone watching. It was a game she often played. She imagined a man stumbling upon her and watching her. She felt his eyes on her like pin pricks, roaming every inch of her body. She rubbed herself in the cooling water. She rubbed her breasts. Then slowly, her fingers dropped between her legs.

Her eyes snapped open when the shudder gripped her. She walked further into the mist to let the water wash her. As soon as she felt the rough creases beneath her feet she stopped. Holding her hair back, she looked for the small crevice in the rocks and then at the bright green slime beyond the crevice. Going down on one knee, she ran her fingers over the crevice and then over the slime. She imagined how it would feel stepping on the slime, the cool slickness that would send her sprawling down the slope of the rocks all the way to the falls and down to the Cobalt Sea.

Daryn stood and backed away. She shook herself and walked out of the mist. Wringing her hair with both hands as she walked back to the boulder, stopped momentarily and scooped up the towel. She walked back across the meadow, past her cabin to the high bluff above the sea. She spread the towel on the grass and sat on it crossed legged.

Leaning back on her hands, she closed her eyes and tilted her face up to the sun. She felt the heat on her face. She let her mind float in the heat. Her mind roamed to thoughts of – the Sad American Falls, of the explorer who discovered it long ago. How did the legend go? The first man to ever lay eyes on the falls, sat down and cried at its beauty. He stayed there for an entire day, dreaming of his home, of a lush green land far far away. Of Earth. Legend had it he was a namer of things, a so man moved by the great beauty of Octavion, he spent his life as a nomad, discovering and naming rivers, mountains, seas and oceans.

She blinked her eyes to the bright sunlight, rolled on her side and lay, face down on the towel. She thought about her home as a little girl. It seemed like so long ago. She remembered the dusty streets of Vermilion Town, of the stone village at the edge of the Cinnamon Hills on the far side of Octavion, across the Silver

Desert. She remembered the stone house her mother and father had built, her room overlooking a narrow street that always smelled of cooked meant and tangy goat yogurt.

She remembered evenings spent playing on the front porch, shielding her eyes to watch the strong sun fall behind the Cinnamon Hills, as long orange and brown shadows crept across Vermilion Town. She remembered days spent playing on the dusty streets, the smell of her mothers pancakes, the sweet taste of cane syrup.

She remembered the warmth of her father's beard on her face. He was the only man who ever loved her, the only man who loved her without reason, without limit. She remembered him hunched over his workbench, the wheel of his sewing machine spinning as he made clothing for the Octavion settlers, practical clothes for a harsh world. Her father was a tailor. He was a frail, gentle man, who crumbled when her mother died.

Daryn was sure the stone house was still there along the dusty streets of a town so far away, it might as well be on another world. She was sure the brown and orange shadows still crawled over her house when the sun fell behind the Cinnamon Hills. She felt a tear on her cheek.

Rising on her hands and knees, she crawled over to the edge of the bluff and lay on the cool grass and looked down at the crystal water. The water was as bright blue close to the beach. Moving away, the water became turquoise with streaks of bright green and purplish blue near the reefs. In the distance, the Cobalt sea was pale blue, so pale it was hard to tell where the sea ended and the sky began.

Daryn watched three Ichthyosaurs moving beneath the waves. They appeared as black stains sliding in the water, their fins breaking the surface as they rolled in the sea. She'd seen an elasmosaurus once, cruising in deeper water, it's hideous head bobbing as it rocked in the water.

A noise below drew Daryn's attention back to the beach. She craned her neck over the side and looked down at two dimetrodons scurrying along the narrow beach. Snapping at one another, their sail fins swayed as they darted back toward the jungle that ran to the right of the bluff.

Shielding her eyes, Daryn looked over at the trees and saw three pterodactyls perched along the tree tops. One spread its leathery wings and jumped from its perch, flapping in jerky motions as it rose and swooped away. Its loud cackle echoed back to Daryn as she looked again at the sea. The strong Octavion sun was beginning its quick descent now, falling toward the sea, streaking the waters with an iridescent glow, turning the horizon into copper.

Daryn rose and stretched and picked up her towel. She walked back to the cabin and felt the depression again in her chest, like a dead heart, like a dead stone in her breast.

"No," she thought, "I won't think about it."

But there was no way she could not think about it. In the morning the hovercraft would return and the men would disembark. She ran her right hand over her left wrist, over the red mark that was still tender, that was always tender. And she fought as hard as she could, to keep from crying. She stayed up later than usual, much later, fighting off the dread.

The hovercraft arrived not long after dark, its ear-piercing hum unmistakable as it banked over the jungle and came to rest between the cabin and the Cobalt Sea. Daryn sat up in bed. She rubbed her temples and tried to calm down. When the engine killed, she jumped up and pulled on a shirt and shorts. She made it into the front room before the door slammed open.

Howard stood in the doorway, a scowl on his bearded face. Daryn retreated to the sofa and sat, her hands pressed against her knees. Howard's black hair was messed, his beard rough looking, dark stains dotted his light green uniform. He leered angrily at her. Daryn felt her heart now, pounding in her chest.

Rubbing his beard with his left hand, Howard began to unzip his jumpsuit as he stepped into the cabin.

"Come on," he said gruffly. "What are you doing wearing clothes?"

A blond head bobbed behind Howard. A pair of blue eyes peeked around Howard's large shoulder as Daryn stood slowly.

"Come on," Howard said, climbing out of his jumpsuit.

Daryn slipped her fingers into the waist band of the shorts and pulled them down. She kicked them aside as the man behind Howard stepped into the room. In the same officer's green jumpsuit, the man stared at Daryn, running his gaze down between her legs.

"Come on!" Howard was naked now and moving toward her.

Daryn pulled her top off and dropped it just as Howard pushed her back on the sofa and mounted her. She squirmed; and he grabbed her throat and squeezed.

His breath reeked of liquor and he smelled of sweat and dirt. Daryn closed her eyes and let herself go limp and thought of the falls and then of cobalt water and cinnamon hills and stone huts and a sky streaked in copper. As soon as Howard finished he rolled off and said, "She's yours."

Daryn looked up at the man who stepped forward and climbed out of his jumpsuit. Smaller and younger than Howard, the man looked much cleaner with a neat beard and eyes that actually stared back at her.

She wasn't sure, but she thought she saw a shy smile and maybe even a hint of embarrassment as he moved between her legs. Far gentler, the man put his hands on her shoulders as he slipped inside her and took his time with her, breathing heavily and actually kissing her mouth before he came.

He climbed off gently and fell back on the floor, his eyes roaming from her breasts to between her legs. Daryn felt the leaking now. She stood up slowly, feeling it roll down her legs.

Howard grabbed her wrist and said, "Food. Bitch!"

When she reached for her shorts, he grabbed them and threw them across the room.

"I like to keep the bitch naked," he told the other man. Daryn could feel them watch as she walked away into the kitchen to the refrigerator. She pulled out two of the pre-formed meals and slid them into the oven.

"No knives in there?" the other man asked Howard.

"Naw. Spoons and forks only. But it's smart to keep an eye on her. She's dangerous."

"How?"

"She's got hands, don't she?"

Howard turned to Daryn and said, "Come back here."

She walked back in.

"Stand there." He motioned that she should stand in front of both of them.

"Now put your hands behind you," Howard said. "Move those feet apart."

Daryn closed her eyes as the men stared at her. Her heart no longer racing, she forced herself to think of the falls again, of the thundering sound of the white water plummeting from Mount Azure. She listened to the timer clicking on the oven and wondered how it would feel to stand naked in front of a man with softer eyes, with eyes that looked at her longingly instead of violently. She had that once, a long time ago, for a short while. She was so young and the time was so short.

The timer finally went off. She moved back into the kitchen and laid out plates for them and pulled their meals from the oven. She drew ale for them and placed goblets next to each of their plates before retreating back into the living room.

"Stay where we can see you, bitch." Howard shoved meat into his mouth, then washed it down with ale.

"Watch that ale," he told the other. "Don't overdo it 'til we strap her down."

The other man looked at Daryn as she sat in a chair where they could see her.

"What's her name?"

"Bitch," Howard said. "Just call her bitch."

Daryn closed her eyes. She listened as they went back to eating, smacking their lips, sucking on the goblets. She heard them talk about two tyrannosaurs they over-flew in the Indigo Forest, and of the stegosaurus herds along the plateau.

"Naw," Howard said. "Nothing can get up on this bluff except those damn pterodactyls. But you can slap those little bastards away."

Howard finished eating first. He shoved his plate aside.

Daryn got up immediately and put it in the cleaner.

"Where'd you find her?" the other man asked, staring at Daryn's butt as she passed.

"Found her in a bar in Tulage."

"Near the ionic mines?"

"Yeah." Howard belched. "Someone told me she lost her man in a cave in or something."

"She never told you."

"She don't talk."

The other man rose and put his plate in the cleaner and said, "I'll get the supplies."

Howard leaned back in his chair and put his hands behind his head.

Daryn watched the other man carry in the pre-formed meals and the other supplies and tired her best not to show any emotion when he dropped the box of books next to her feet.

"The boys sent these," he said, nodding to the books. "My name's Jason," the man said. He shrugged and headed back into the kitchen to refill his goblet with ale.

Rising, Howard waved to Daryn and said, "Come on, Bitch."

She followed him down the hall. He pointed to the bathroom and said, "Go ahead."

He watched her from the hall.

Then he followed her into the room and put her in bed, snapping the steel manacle on her left wrist. He checked to make sure the manacle was still secured to the steel headboard before leaving her.

Daryn listened to the men drink their ale and tell their stories. She heard pieces of the conversation. Jason called Howard's set up here "perfect." Howard said something about "a man draining himself." When they laughed they sounded like young pterodactyls on their first flight.

After a few minutes, Daryn reached over to the paperback book on the table next to the bed and looked at it. It was an earth book, aged and worn, with an exotic scene of the interior of a cafe on its cover. There were three characters in the scene. In the foreground sat a man with gray hair and a moustache. He was pouring himself a cup of liquid from a golden carafe. The man looked very much like Daryn's father. There was a determined look on the man's hawk-like face.

Behind and to the left of the man who looked like Daryn's father stood an exotic looking woman with long brown hair. The woman was dressed in lacy white shoulder epaulets and a matching brassiere. Around her waist was a white belt that held up a long white scarf that draped between her shapely legs. She also wore tall white high heel shoes. The woman danced atop a small dance floor made of white light that illuminated her from the floor up. Daryn wondered what it would be like to wear shoes with such high heels.

Between the two characters stood another character. This was the main character of the book. Young and rugged looking, with reddish hair, his name was Marid. He stood in the open doorway of the cafe, looking out at a street scene, at a narrow street of sand colored buildings. He was a kind man in an unkind world, a gentle man, a caring man.

This was the third book in an old Earth series. She ran her fingers over the title – *The Exile Kiss* by George Alec Effinger. She enjoyed these books so much because she liked the women. They were so independent. She also liked the way the people could alter their lives and personalities by plugging in mind-altering devices directly into their skulls. She longed to alter herself. She longed to be lost in an exotic cafe.

Daryn read two chapters, then put the book back. She didn't want to rush it. She wanted to savor every scene, to read the book ever so slowly. She was just readjusting herself when she saw Howard standing at the foot of the bed. Rubbing his hairy chest, he nodded to her legs and said, "Open them up." She closed her eyes and pretended she was in a cafe and a man like Marid was staring at her.

When Howard was finished with her, he rolled over and went to sleep. Jason climbed on her immediately, his breath now laced with the bittersweet scent of strong ale. Suspending himself above her on his hands and knees, Jason craned his neck down and kissed her again on the mouth and took his time with her, took a long long time.

Jason fell asleep on the other side of Daryn, sandwiching her against Howard's sweaty back. They didn't even turn off the light. She closed her eyes and tried to sleep. She let her mind roam to a far away land, an city of lights and dancing girls and people who were not who they were supposed to be, people who were someone else.

Much later, she felt Jason climb on her again and start up again. She pretended to sleep, but his jerking hurt her arm so much she had to readjust herself.

"Oh," Jason said. He grabbed her arm and looked at it. "Does it hurt?"

Daryn didn't meet his gaze, but she nodded.

Jason grunted and climbed off. He went into the front room and came back with Howard's large set of keys. It took a few tries, but he found the key and unlocked the manacle. Still holding it shut, he paused and said, "Howard warned me not to let you out."

Daryn waited.

"You'll be a good girl, now won't you?"

Daryn turned her gaze to him and nodded slowly.

As soon as he let her out, she rubbed her wrist. It was so raw it was blood red. She climbed out of bed.

"Where are you going?" Jason asked anxiously.

She went into the bathroom.

"Oh," he said, but didn't follow.

Stepping back into the hall, she looked at Jason and raised her right hand and waved him forward. Then she turned and went down the hall, through the living room and out the front door. She waited out on the porch for Jason who appeared in the doorway two seconds later.

"Wait. What are you doing?" Jason's said in a harsh whisper. He didn't want to wake Howard.

Daryn looked up at the bright stars in the cloudless, black sky. The wind shifted, and a fine sprinkle of mist floated over them from the falls. It felt so cool on Daryn's body. She turned back to Jason and forced herself to smile. She reached her hand out. He took it and she led him around the cabin and through the meadow for the falls. The falls loomed like a monstrous ghost in the starlight, its roar echoing in Daryn's ears as she led Jason past the boulders and into the mist.

The water swirled around Daryn, washing the sweat off her body, washing the pain away from her wrist, cleaning her so completely. She rubbed her hands over her body. Facing the mist, she pulled her hair back and let the water flow over her face.

Jason stood near the edge of the mist. Hesitating, he looked back toward the cabin. When he turned back to Daryn, she opened her arms for him. He moved slowly to her. He had trouble keeping his balance on the rocks. Daryn wrapped her arms around his neck and kissed his lips and then pulled away, further into the mist.

She heard him trying to yell over the roar of the waterfalls, but could not understand. Still facing him, she reached her hands out and he took them and slowly, ever so slowly, she led him deeper into the water. She was having trouble catching her breath in the falling water, and struggled to keep her footing. She continued to smile at Jason and continued to pull him along. She felt the rough creases underfoot now and swung her foot in a slow arch until she found the crevice.

Daryn planted her right heel firmly in the crevice, let go of Jason's hand and then pretended to fall. Jason reached for her. Daryn pulled away, grabbing the crevice with both hands, letting her feet and body slide over the slime toward the falls.

Jason leaned forward and reached again. Daryn reached her left hand out. When he grabbed her hand, she pulled hard. His feet hit the slime and slipped out from under him, slamming him hard on the rocks. Daryn pulled her hand away and watched Jason struggle, watched him squirm, spreading his hands and feet out. The more he struggled, the faster he slid. Shoved along by the water, he slid all the way down to the edge and then over the side of the cliff.

She thought she heard him scream but only for an instant.

Daryn pulled herself away from the slime. Planting her feet in the crevice, she pushed herself away to crawl back out of the mist. She pulled her hair back again and waited to catch her breath before hurrying back across the meadow.

She eased into the front room, pulled on her shirt and shorts and dug into Jason's pockets for his keys. Fumbling them, she froze and listened for Howard. Three heartbeats later, she slipped back out of the cabin and bolted for the hovercraft.

There werc too many keys. Daryn struggled with each, looking back at the open door of the cabin between gasping breaths. A noise overhead made her drop the keys. She recognized the sound of leathery wings as pterodactyls passed overhead.

She looked back at the door again, fumbled with the keys and kept trying. Finally, a key slipped into the lock. She turned it and it opened. Then a loud scream knocked Daryn back. She fell down and saw, perched on the hovercraft, the hunched brown body of a pterodactyl. It opened its long jaws and screeched again.

Daryn looked back at the cabin and then ran her hands over the ground until she found a rock. Rising, she threw the rock at the pterodactyl, catching it square in its chest, sending it tumbling backward off the hovercraft. It screamed loudly as it flapped off into the night.

Daryn opened the door of the hovercraft and heard another sound. She turned just as Howard jumped off the porch and raced right for her. Daryn fell away from the hovercraft, turned and ran around it and headed straight for the falls. She heard Howard's footfalls behind her as she raced across the meadow.

Without looking back, without decreasing her pace, she ran headlong for the falls and noticed, as she reached the boulders, the faint gray rays of dawn. She ran into the mist, turned to her left quickly and tried her best to slow down. She fell and tumbled on the rock and finally came to a stop well into the waterfall. She looked back for Howard, but couldn't see him.

Gasping for breath, she crawled backward along the rock toward the falls, her arms and feet spread wide until she felt the creases under her left foot and eased over. She found the crevice, planted both feet in it and waited.

She hadn't even caught her breath when he came through the water for her. Moving slowly and sure-footed in his work boots, Howard reached for her. Daryn slid back, grabbing the crevice with both hands. Howard lunged for her and grabbed her just as his feet hit the slime and gave out from under him. He crashed on her, tearing her hands away from the crevice. The force of his weight shoved them apart. But Daryn was on the slime now and felt herself slipping, felt the cascading water pushing her along the slope of the huge cliff down toward the falls.

She saw Howard sliding too, away from her but also for the falls. Struggling, he slid faster and faster. Daryn clawed at the slime, tried her best to dig her fingernails, her toenails, to bite at the slime, anything to slow her descent.

But the water poured on her and the slime pulled at her and finally, in one sinking moment her legs fell away and she plummeted over the side and down the long waterfall. Her breath was gone. Her body seemed to rise for an instant and then seemed to fly as she sank and fell and fell. Daryn opened her eyes and reached her arms out and thought – so this is what it feels like to die.

She closed her eyes and time went away.

Until – she felt a sudden warmth.

Until she tasted something salty.

Until she broke the surface and opened her eyes again in the Cobalt Sea.

It took a few seconds to distinguish the falls in front of her, the churning columns of water rising from the sea in giant spurts. Instinctively she pushed back away from the churning water and something touched her foot.

Ichthyosaur.

Daryn jumped to the side and saw – a hand. Howard rose from the water and coughed into Daryn's face and then gasped. He coughed again and Daryn turned and swam, pulling herself with her aching arms, pushing herself with her legs, pushing herself away from the falls, and away from him.

Only, the falls sucked her back. She felt herself slid back toward the bubbling water. She pulled harder with her arms, sank a moment and then shot forward, propelled with the water away from the falls. She swallowed water this time and struggled to catch her breath. She rolled on her back and coughed and felt the sun on her face now, the wonderful warm sun.

Rubbing her eyes, she looked around quickly. He wasn't there. She dipped under the water and looked through the crystalline water. Nothing. And slowly she made her way around the bluff to the narrow beach. The wet sand was gritty under her hands. She pulled herself up and crawled away from the water and collapsed. She turned her head to the side and felt the sun again on her eyelids and her cheek and lips.

Dimetrodons.

She tried to open her eyes, but they wouldn't open. She told herself she had to open her eyes. She had to get up off the beach. She told herself again – *dimetrodons.* Her right eye struggled to open. She licked her lips and pushed herself up off the wet sand, sat up, looked around at the empty beach. The sea was also empty and beautiful, shimmering in the sunlight.

Her entire body ached, as if she'd been pounded. She took cautious steps, watching her legs and moving her arms around. Nothing seemed broken. She ran her fingers over her face and pulled her hair back once again.

At the base of the bluff, she shaded her eyes with her hands and looked up. It wasn't a sheer face, but it was very steep. There were, however bushes and vines and rocks. Looking around again for dimetrodons, she saw none and started up the cliff. The vines smelled sweetly of chlorophyll.

She had risen about six feet when she felt something grab her ankle. Instinctively she clung to the vines and kicked furiously and looked down into Howard's face. Twisted and blue, the face was contorted in anger. He opened his mouth and screamed, "Bitch!"

Howard lifted his right fist and hammered her calf. Pain shot up the leg. Daryn pulled on the vines and tried kicking herself free as Howard raised his fist again. She heard a growl. No, it was a snarl, a long hissing snarl.

Howard stopped. His head turned away. Daryn kicked his hand with her other foot; and he let go. She clambered up and then saw them, on the beach.

Two dimetrodons moved along the beach, hissing and snarling as they crept toward Howard. Their sail fins swaying, their dagger teeth bared, the twelve foot monsters rose on their toes and then raced for Howard. They were so *fast*. Howard climbed a few feet before the first one struck, sinking its teeth into Howard's leg and pulling him down.

His hideous scream was muffled quickly as the second dimetrodon struck, ripping Howard's left arm off at the shoulder. Twisting their strong necks as they tore at the flesh, the dimetrodons lifted their heads and swallowed large pieces of Howard until all that was left was one leg, which they fought over. The ripped it in two, swallowed it down and then took a snip out of one another, their faces masked in blood. Racing back on to the sand, their heads jerked from side to side as they searched for anything else they could eat. The sun glimmered off their fins as they darted back and forth across the white sand.

Daryn caught her breath, looked up and slowly ascended the cliff. A pterodactyl swooped close by, but she saw it coming and threw a stick at it. She took her time, carefully setting each foot before moving up until she was at last near the top of the bluff. She threw her right hand up and dug into the grass and pulled herself up, was in mid-pull when a hand grabbed her and yanked her up in one fell swoop.

Daryn tumbled over Jason and landed on her back on the other side of the man. Shielding her eyes again from the sun, she tensed up and inched away from him. But Jason did not move. He glared at her with a face swollen and misshapen. His left arm dangled at an hideous angle from his shoulder. Grass stains marked his good arm and his face.

On his knees now, Jason opened his mouth and tried to speak but nothing came out. He looked at her with such a pitiful look, not angry or violent, but sad and pitiful. He whimpered and sank back.

Daryn rose and moved around Jason and gave him a good kick and watched him tumble over the edge of the bluff. She leaning over the crest to see him slam against the sides of the cliff, all the way to the beach. The dimetrodons, six now, raced for Jason. They ripped him apart and devoured his body in furious seconds.

The sun was at its height when Daryn stepped walked naked out of the mist of the Sad American Falls and strolled back across the meadow to the cabin. She put on a white cotton blouse and soft denim shorts and leather boots, she picked up the last of her bags and the two sacks of food she'd prepared, along with the water containers. She put them in the hovercraft next to her boxes of worn paperbacks. She made sure she had all her paperbacks.

Daryn went back into the cabin and poured kerosene on the bed and down the hall and on the sofa and in the kitchen all the way out to the front porch. She tossed the metal container back on the porch before striking a match.

Holding the match over the porch, she said, "Goodbye."

She dropped the match and backed away.

The cabin burned beneath the strong Octavion sun, flames rising, smoke billowing. Daryn felt no heat on her face, no heat whatsoever. The wind had shifted and blew in from the east, bringing sheets of mist from the falls, mist that touched her face and clung to her arms. She looked at the falls and Mount Azure towering overhead and at the magnificence of the Perfume Mountains.

The hovercraft started right up. Gently prodding its controls, Daryn rose over the burning cabin and skirted the falls before turning to circle the mountains. She set a course for the badlands of the Silver Desert and the rolling Cinnamon Hills beyond and the familiar shadows and dusty streets of home.

THE END *of* "A Hot and Copper Sky"

This story is for my friend George Alec Effinger

Slimy Things Did Crawl With Legs Upon The Slimy Sea

The very deep did rot: O Christ!
That ever this should be!
Yea, slimy things did crawl with legs
Upon the slimy sea.

"The Rime of the Ancient Mariner"
Samuel Taylor Coleridge (Earth, 1798 a.d.)

Dimetrodons were already on the beach, basking in the morning sun. Using their sail-fins like radiators, they waited patiently for the sun to warm their cool blood, so they could rush back into the jungle to feed on the slower reptiles, still groggy from the chilly night.

Andrew sat on the large, flat rock at the edge of the low cliff and watched the dinosaurs as they slowly awoke on the white beach across the narrows from his small island. He took a sip of coffee from the mug cradled between his rough hands and smiled as the dimetrodons, one by one, seemed to jump-start and hurry back into the bush. He tried tracing their path through the jungle but lost sight of each as soon as the dinosaur slipped into the foliage.

One of the baskers eventually noticed him and began moving his way but he paid it no mind. Dimetrodons could not swim, not even across the narrows that separated Andrew's island from the mainland.

He was thinking of going back for more coffee when he heard the screen door slam. Turning, he watched Kate step off the back porch. She was wearing his oversized terry-cloth robe and carrying a mug in one hand and the coffee pot in the other. Barefoot, she tiptoed across the cool grass.

When she arrived, she poured him a fresh cup and then noticed the dimetrodons.

"Oh, wow!"

"Hey, don't spill it on me."

"Sorry," she said, glancing at his cup before turning back to the occupants of the beach.

"Ever see any this close before?"

"No!" She quickly sat on the next rock and pulled her knees up against her chest.

Kate had red hair, like her mother. She also had her mother's dark green eyes. But she had his brother's stubborn streak. She was Andrew's niece, Andrew's only living relative.

"A couple years ago," he said, "I watched two big ones attack a smaller one. They only get about twelve feet long. But those long teeth. It was a pretty gruesome sight."

He remembered how the larger ones had cornered the small, weaker one on the beach. They attacked separately, lashing out and ripping at the little one who'd fought as best it could, twisting and biting back. It did not take long for a scarlet streak to surface on the flank of the smaller one, glistening beneath the strong sun. The sand became muddy with blood. The smaller one grew drunk from weakness, and the two larger ones moved in for the kill.

A feeding frenzy immediately followed. Propelled by strong legs moving in unison, right legs first and then left legs moving together, muscles bulging beneath the shiny green skin, a host of dimetrodons rushed from the bush for their piece of flesh. Dagger length teeth slashed the corpse. Hungry mouths ripped away the meat, heads shaking like mad dogs to dislodge a mouthful, until all that was left was a bloody heap at the edge of the water. Then the hatchlings came running out of the jungle for their share. The big ones snapped at the little ones, but the hatchlings were too fast to be caught. The original battle had taken a hour; the feast, ten minutes at most.

"When the tide's out," he told her, pointing to the narrows, "you can see ichthyosaurs cruising below. Once I saw an elasmosaurus. Big, snake head rising out of the water like a damn dragon. Black eyes, long teeth sticking out of both sides of its ugly mouth."

2

Kate looked down at the water for a moment and then back at the dimetrodons. When her uncle didn't notice, she peeked at him. He didn't look anything like her father. Andrew had a craggy face and a full mane of white hair. He was much darker, but that was probably from a life in the sun. Then again, she barely remembered her father.

She wondered if there was anything else she could do to convince the old man to leave. Deep down, she knew he would never leave. The last twenty-four hours had confirmed it. Rising, she bent over and kissed her uncle on top of his head. Then she went back into the house to finish packing.

3

She's prettier than her mother, Andrew was thinking, even with her glasses. She was nicer too. He was still amazed that she had come. Out of the blue, literally, she dropped from a helicopter with a chip on her shoulder and a determination that she would save him, convince him to leave.

He would never forget how wide her eyes looked when she pulled off her glasses and said, "Hello, Uncle Andrew. I've come to save you."

The last dimetrodon ran back into the jungle, leaving a spray of sand in its wake. All that was left were the footprints and the tail prints. Andrew stood up, stretched and poured the remainder of his coffee into the narrows.

He found Kate on the front porch. She looked prim in her khaki jump suit, her neat suitcase packed and waiting next to her small feet. She was scanning the wide expanse of the Celadon Sea on the windward side of the island. This was an amazing sea, its water a shade of light green known to artists as 'celadon'. She had a hand over her eyes to shield them from the glare off the pale turquoise water. The early morning sun on Octavion, especially along the southern hemisphere, was much harsher than the old sun of Earth.

"See anything?" he asked.

"No, not yet." She pulled her hand away and said, "Is it always like this?"

"Yep."

"It's so beautiful," she admitted.

He looked at the sea and knew what she felt, gazing at the glittering, pale green water. Off to his right he caught sight of three pterodactyls heading out over the water. Unlike the graceful water eagles of Earth, the pterodactyls did not soar. They darted like bats freed from a monstrous cave.

Kate also saw them and asked, "Pteranodons?"

"No, pterodactyls. Little bastards. There are no pteranodons in this hemisphere."

"Oh."

4

Kate looked down at the small, air-powered fog horn clipped to her uncle's belt and remembered what he'd said when she'd asked about it. "I use it to shoo away the damn pterodactyls, the pesky bastards." He also told her, "No use wasting a bullet on them. They're too tough to eat. Can't even use the meat as bait, unless you're fishing for ichthyosaurs or tylosaurs."

She thought about that statement. It sounded like something a man of the wilderness would say. Twenty years alone in the wild gave him that right, she figured. Then she remembered an even more succinct statement he'd made about how to avoid being eaten by a dinosaur. It summed up her uncle's life in one smooth sentence.

He said, "Don't put yourself out as a meal and they won't eat you."

She looked back at the sky and asked another question, "Ever see one of those giant ones, the quetza . . .?"

"Quetzalcoatlus," he said with a smile. "Naw, they're extinct."

5

Andrew heard the outboard and glanced at his watch. They were on time, all right. He moved to the edge of the cliff to watch the long boat moor against the stone steps he had carved into the front cliff of his island. For a moment he thought to yell down to the coast guardsmen to watch their step, to watch out for the moss on the steps and the ditches at the top of the cliff, but grown up guardsmen should be able to negotiate such small obstacles.

He turned back to his niece. She was staring at him, her glasses in her hand, her eyes wide and moist.

6

Kate knew the final minute would be the roughest. No sense in asking him again to leave. He would never leave his damn island. She felt a tear running down her face and wiped it away quickly. She started to turn, but he did something unexpected.

He reached over and wrapped his arms around her and hugged her. It happened too fast for her to react. She stood stiffly in his arms and waited.

"You know," he whispered in her ear, "I never much liked my brother. Never much liked your mother either. But you, I always liked you. From the first day I saw you."

Kate felt a swelling in her chest and eased her stance to hug him back. She tried saying something funny, "I was an infant. Everybody likes babies."

"No. I could tell even then that you were different. I told your mother that you were probably the only special person in their entire family. Know what she said?"

Kate shook her head no.

"She told me to put you down before I dropped and killed you."

That sounded like her mother.

7

Andrew squeezed her again. He was still amazed that she had come. It made him feel different and strange. Then he whispered again in her ear, whispered something he hadn't said in a long, long time, "Thank you."

She leaned back and asked, "For what?"

"For coming."

She pulled away and headed for her suitcase. He wasn't sure, but her eyes looked wet.

Andrew greeted the two guardsmen, who were in a big hurry. Only one spoke, the one with blond hair. He looked about twenty, exactly Kate's age. Probably didn't even shave. But Andrew was glad to see them, glad they came to take his niece to safety.

Kate handed her suitcase to the other guardsman and announced she would be the only one going.

"Everyone east of the Perfume Mountains has to evacuate," the blond guardsman stated.

"I'm not leaving," Andrew said.

"We won't be back. As soon as we get to our ship, we're sailing."

"Good."

"Is it that close?" Kate asked.

"It'll be here tomorrow," the guardsman answered dryly.

Kate looked at the sea again. "There's nothing," she said.

The blond guardsman picked up her suitcase and said, "It's already crossed the Indigo Sea and the Cinnamon Plains. It'll be here tomorrow."

"Well," she said, turning once again to her uncle, "I guess I'll see you when I see you."

He smiled at her. "Don't worry about me. I'm too ornery to die."

Kate nodded and then led the way down to the boat. Andrew watched from above. As the boat pulled away, he went back through his house to the low cliff out back and watched them round the isle and pass through the narrows.

Kate looked up at him from the boat. He waved and she waved back, hesitantly. He felt a welling of emotion in his throat as the boat passed and Kate's face turned away for the last time. Then the motor stopped and she looked up at him again. She started laughing. Andrew didn't laugh.

"Watch out," he yelled. "You're heading for the beach!"

The blond guardsman waved him off and joined his comrade trying to restart the engine.

Andrew cupped his hands around his mouth and shouted, "Don't beach it!"

The guardsmen weren't listening.

He searched the jungle as best he could, inching toward the edge of the cliff. When he spotted a dimetrodon's fin, he wheeled and ran back into his house for his rifle. He heard screams on his way back. Somehow, the dimetrodon had latched on to the blond guardsman and was dragging the screaming man across the beach. The other guardsman was firing a hand gun into the dimetrodon, point blank.

Andrew was more concerned about the two other dimetrodons rushing out on the beach, straight for the fresh blood. He felled both of them in rapid succession. But three more quickly followed out of the jungle. He took aim and yelled at the same time, "Jump in the water! Jump in the water!"

His next shot missed and the remaining guardsman was caught.

"Jump!" he screamed to his niece. "They can't swim!"

Kate dove into the water.

He dropped the gun and ran to the rock steps along the low cliff. He slipped on the moss and tumbled into the water. His back hurt immediately, his left arm felt numb, and his knee felt as if it had been torn in two. Pulling hard with his right arm and kicking with his good knee, he managed to move toward Kate who was rapidly crossing the narrows. He bore down and lengthened his stroke. Looking up momentarily, he barely had time to avoid being overrun by his niece.

She grabbed his neck and pulled him down, wrapping her legs around his chest. She was panicked and he needed all his might to keep them both up. Grabbing the front of her jump suit, he twisted her around and began back-peddling for his island. Kate continued struggling. Her savage beating at the water aided their forward motion.

Andrew shoved her up on the first step and paused to catch his breath. Immediately, she clawed at his shirt to pull him from the water. He climbed up and grabbed her and shook her.

She coughed in his face and said, "Ichthyosaurs!"

He looked back but the water was empty. "Where?" he said.

She blinked at him and then stared at the water with her mouth open. He tucked his right arm under her and helped her up the stairs, carefully.

"Don't," he told her when she raised her head to look back at the beach. He pushed her head down with his left arm, which caused him to wince in pain. He did not stop until he deposited her on the back porch. Then he went back for his rifle. His left arm ached like hell but seemed to be functioning. His left knee was bleeding and would have to be mended. It burned but still supported his weight. His back ached with a deep, dull pain.

He took a look at the beach before picking up the rifle. He counted twelve dimetrodons feasting on the carcasses of the dead guardsmen.

After wrapping a towel around his knee, Andrew poured Kate a hot bath and led her into the bathroom. Her face was waxen and she wouldn't look into his eyes, but eventually she began to remove her jump suit. He closed the door on his way out and went straight for the first aid kit in his kitchen.

8

Kate soaked in the tub until the water went cool. Then she emptied it and ran another tub full of hot water and soaked some more. She tried to put it out of her mind, but every time she closed her eyes, she saw the dagger teeth and all the blood. When her second tub went cold, she emptied it and took a shower to wash her hair, and to wash away the memory. Her hair was easily cleaned. It would take much more to erase that memory. After drying herself, she pulled on the terry cloth robe hanging inside the door.

Her uncle was in the living room, surrounded by large red containers that had *kerosene* marked on their sides. Several larger white containers behind him had the word *acid* on them. She noticed he was favoring his left knee.

"You're hurt?"

He looked up from his bent position and put a hand on his back as he rose. "Naw. Just a scratch. How are you doing?"

She nodded and looked away from his searching eyes. She noticed two flame throwers next to the sofa. He really was going to fight it.

"I've got CO2 guns also," he said, pointing to a row of oversized fire extinguishers lined inside the front door.

She still felt a little weak so she sat on the sofa and asked, "Is this going to be enough?"

"All we need is twenty-four hours."

He was quoting the legend. Andrew pointed to the other end of the sofa and said, "I found some things you can put on." Then he went back to work.

After a minute, she got up and took the clothes into the bathroom. Her bra and panties were dry enough. The shirt he gave her was too big and so were the pants, but the rope belt held them up. Still barefoot, she went out on the front porch and hung her jump suit on the rail next to her shoes and socks. She could hear Andrew in the shower now, so she went to her room and curled up in bed and waited. She tried not to close her eyes, afraid she would see the blood again. Her uncle came in a while later with some thick syrup and said, "Come on, take some of this?"

"What is it?"

"Medicine."

"I'm not hurt."

He nodded and took a spoon full himself. She sat up and took some also. "I'll be up in a minute," she told him on his way out. The next thing she remembered, her uncle woke her up, placing her dry jump suit and shoes on the foot of her bed.

The sun was just setting in the distant sky, sinking into the Celadon Sea. Kate joined her uncle out on the front porch. She strained her eyes, looking for the slime, but could see nothing except the golden sun, sizzling on the horizon.

"It'll be here in the morning," he said.

She looked into his eyes and asked, "How can you be sure?"

"It's the legend." Then he turned and added, "Come on in. It's supper time."

She helped him with the meal. Only she didn't want to know what kind of meat they were eating. She knew it would taste good, like the previous night's fish but she didn't want to know what she was eating.

They dined in silence at a table her uncle had built by hand, sitting on chairs he had constructed from the wood he had carried from the jungle. By candlelight, they ate in the airy log house her uncle had built, piece by piece, the warm sea breeze flowing through the open doors from the Celadon Sea.

The meal was delicious, especially the marinated meat her uncle had prepared. She passed on the strong homemade beer and opted for the wild tea. She helped him clean up the dishes, dishes that would probably be gone the next morning. No, she told herself, the slime only destroys organic material. The wooden house would be gone and they would be gone, but the ceramic dishes would remain, along with the silverware and the empty containers of CO_2.

As he'd done the previous evening, Andrew went out on the front porch with his pipe. She fixed coffee and joined him with two steamy cups. He thanked her but said nothing else until the coffee was finished and his pipe was out. Andrew looked tired. His deep set eyes stared out to sea, his jaw fixed. He looked ready for the following day. Only he looked old.

Rising, he said, "We'd better get some sleep."

"Can we light the fireplace?" she asked.

"Sure."

9

An hour later, the warmth from the stone fireplace filled the house. Kate lay on the sofa, watching the flames. Andrew was on the floor next to the fire, poking it with a metal rod.

"If this was a steel shuttered house, we'd have no problem," she heard herself say.

"You don't get fireplaces in prefab houses," he said, replacing the poker and leaning back on the wooly rug.

He closed his eyes and said, "I cut each log of this place by hand, not with a chain saw, but with an ax. One by one. I dragged them through the bush and then rafted them across the narrows.

"It took me over a year to close in the house. It took me five more to finish it."

"You didn't build the refrigerator," she told him.

"Nope. The supply boat brought it, just like it brings my coffee and tobacco. Nothing wrong with borrowing a little civilization, like bullets and hot water heaters and generators."

"Everything but people, huh?"

She was spunky, all right. He was glad she sounded like her old self.

"Uh huh, everything but people," he said.

They remained quiet for a while until she asked about the slime. "What's it like? I mean, I only heard the legend. But it's . . . it's so frightening."

He answered in a voice that was low and distant. "It will come like a glacier. Like a foul fungus. From the Indigo Sea, across the Celadon Sea. It will eat everything until it is gorged and then it will die within the scent of the Perfume Mountains."

She'd heard all that before. So, he didn't know anything about the slime that she didn't know. Yet, he was surprisingly calm. He was probably doing that on purpose, she figured, to calm her.

"Uncle Andrew, how'd you cut the trees with all the dimetrodons in the forest?"

He turned to her with that soft look in his eyes and shrugged. "Don't put yourself out as a meal and they won't eat you. That, and a good rifle helps."

The fire felt good on Andrew's face. It made him drowsy. He reached for the drowsiness and tried very hard to fall asleep.

Kate closed her eyes to the heat and waited.

They both waited.

10

When Kate woke, the sun was high. She jumped up and ran out on the front porch and stood next to her uncle. He already had a flame thrower on his back. He was staring at the sea. When she saw it, she gasped.

"Exactly," her uncle said.

Kate leaned against the porch rail, mesmerized by the sight before her. The entire sea was covered in a black veil. It looked like an ocean of death.

Andrew passed her the binoculars. She focused them and, for the first time, saw the slime up close, saw the oozing goo. She had to do a double take because of the jerky movements of the slime. Across the top, things with legs were running, black things with slimy legs.

"I already poured the acid in the first ditch," he said, "and the kerosene in the second."

"Why didn't you wake me?"

"For what?" He waved to the encroaching blackness and said, "For this?"

Kate reached for the other flame thrower.

"There's coffee on the stove," he told her as she donned the apparatus. "You'll have time for coffee," he added.

She did have time for a hot cup, barely. Returning to the porch, there was no need for binoculars anymore. The slime was almost to the island now. Kate watched, as if hypnotized, at the flow of the black muck as it advanced.

11

Andrew walked over to the edge of the front cliff to get a better look. When the slime reached the shore, it began to work its way up the grassy walls and the moss-covered steps. He backed away as it approached. He jumped the acid ditch and then the kerosene trench and waited. In seconds, the goo topped the ridge and slid into the acid ditch. A loud screeching sent Andrew reeling as the advancing slime boiled in the acid.

"Cover your eyes," he warned Kate but there was no need. The wind, for a change, blew from the mainland, carrying the smoke away from them. But the high pitched screeching persisted, gaining in intensity as more slime fell into the pit. Then the screaming died away as quickly as it had started. The smoke cleared, revealing an acid pit overrun by the slime. The goo pushed forward, straight for them.

Andrew lit his torch and waited until the slime oozed into the kerosene ditch before touching it off. A wall of flame shot into the sky, roaring loud enough to seal off the screeching.

12

Kate held her breath as the flame grew in intensity, fed by the slime itself. Maybe, just maybe, she thought, it would continue to burn all the way back to the horizon. But the flame soon diminished and slackened enough for her to see the slime beyond, still pushing forward. She lit her thrower and braced herself.

When the first break in the flame occurred and the black slime slithered through, her uncle stepped over to burn it back. Kate took up position at the other corner of the house and zapped another break in the flame. Each blast of fire scared the slime into gray powder, but only for a minute. The powder gave way to fresh slime, advancing, always advancing. Glancing back at her uncle, Kate saw him keeping three breaks held back. Torching her lone break again, she saw another break form to her right and immediately plugged it with a stream of fire. She could hear the screeching again. It was frightening.

13

When a slimy thing with legs raced forward, toward the house, Andrew jumped over and stomped it into the ground. It popped and hissed beneath his boot. So he stomped it again. Then he plugged the new hole with his flame. They were holding on until the trench went out, like a candle snuffed in the wind. Andrew took a step back and paused. Kate followed suit. When the slime crossed the trench he sprayed it in a wide arch and she did the same. But it was no use.

Andrew bore down and defiantly moved forward, switching to the second canister on his back pack. He continued advancing even as the heat burned at his face. Then a slime jumped at him and landed on his bare arm. It burned so badly, he fell back and tried to pull it off, but it wouldn't budge. He stumbled to the porch and grabbed one of the CO_2 guns and sprayed the slimy thing on his arm, which caused it to fall away immediately. He sprayed his arm again to numb the pain.

Kate ran toward him and threw a wide spray of flame at the encroaching slime. "What happened?" she yelled.

"Don't let it touch you!" He shouted back as he stood and relit his thrower. "It *burns!*"

Side by side they pumped fire at the slime, keeping it away from the house until the throwers were exhausted. Andrew threw his empty pack at the slime and then pulled Kate's off and threw it. He glared at the ooze, which kept coming.

14

Kate already had a CO_2 gun in hand and passed another to Andrew as they fell back on the porch. But the fight seemed to be lost in her uncle. She swooshed the icy CO_2 at the slime, causing it to withdraw momentarily, but Andrew just stood there as if it was over.

"There," she pointed to Andrew's left and said, "hit it there."

He didn't move. He just stared out at the black death.

When the first runner hit her leg, she froze it off with a shot of CO_2, but it burned nonetheless. A second one got her on the wrist. She zapped it too and watched in horror as three jumped on her uncle's legs.

That brought the fight back into the man. Andrew sprayed his legs and began to attack back with the CO_2. But now, the runners were everywhere, racing from the mass of slime to latch on to the railing of the porch, to the floorboards, to the wall of the house and to the two fighters.

In one cataclysmic charge, dozens of runners slammed against the porch. A massed assault, like a volley of hot lead, elicited a fountain of CO_2, sending Andrew and Kate stumbling back into the house. Andrew slammed the door behind them before falling next to his niece.

15

His neck and arms and legs were ablaze. The slime ate at him but Kate was worse. It was on her face and he used his CO_2 to freeze them, and then he pulled them off. Rolling her over, he sprayed the entire length of her body before turning the spray on himself.

It took a few seconds for his eyes to clear from the pain. He rolled Kate back over and saw that she was breathing. The slime had left burn marks on her cheek and neck and both arms, but she was alive.

Then he heard a high pitched scratching along the front wall of his house. He looked and the walls were melting. The slime now blacked out the wide windows. He stumbled to his feet and struggled to the back door and saw that it too was smoldering.

"No!" he screamed. *"No!"* He ran for the CO2, grabbed one and blasted the front wall. He fired the canister until it was empty. Acid smoke belched back into his face, sending him reeling and coughing. The house was filled with the burning smoke.

Falling back next to Kate, he summoned all his strength to pull her to the center of the floor. Then he yanked back the wooly rug and unlatched the wooden door to the storm shelter. He reached in, flipped on the light and then put Kate across his shoulder and went down the steep stone steps. At least there was no moss to trip him.

He put her on the cot at the rear of the shelter and raced back up for the CO2 guns. He grabbed the lot and fell back to the steps. Looking once again at the front wall of his house, he could see hints of dull daylight through the gaping holes the slime had created. Andrew shut the shelter door behind him and bolted it before hurrying down the steps. Pulling everything away from the base of the steps, he dragged it all to the back of the shelter. He flipped on the back light, lined up the CO2 guns, and waited.

16

Kate felt herself waking. Her face burned and her neck burned and her legs ached. She sat up and grabbed her uncle's back. He jumped.

Looking around, she asked hoarsely, "Where are we?"

"Storm shelter," Andrew answered. He tried forcing a smile on his face but couldn't. He managed to croak out, "How about some water?"

"Yeah."

He stepped over to one of the large water bottles, grabbed a porcelain cup and poured her a long, cool drink. Then he poured himself one.

Then they waited.

The water cooled her throat. She wanted more and insisted on getting it herself. Looking around, she could see the narrow chamber was filled with goods, primarily food stuffs and bottled water. She brought him another cupful and sat next to him.

The smoke was the first sign that the shelter door was melting. Her uncle moved forward with a CO2 gun and waited. The slime did not disappoint them. It rolled down the steps, like rotted glue. When it neared the bottom, Andrew began to spray it and continued spraying until his gun was empty.

Kate passed him another and then another and then another. She fed him CO2 guns until there was only one left, then she tapped his shoulder and pulled him back with her into the back corner. Andrew pushed her behind him and withdrew a revolver from the holster on his hip. She hadn't noticed it before, but she knew what it meant. He put the revolver on the cot and waited.

The slime was frozen solid along the bottom of the steps. For a minute, Kate thought that it wasn't going to continue. A runner raced across the top of the frozen ooze and ran into the side wall and stuck there. A couple more runners followed and ended the same way, stuck to the side walls or to the stone floor.

Then a mass of slime moved over the frozen muck at the bottom of the steps and began to advance across the room. Andrew reached for the revolver. But Kate grabbed his arm and pointed to the slime. It had stopped. Kate rubbed her eyes to be sure but the slime advanced no more.

They both held their breaths for a long, heart-stammering minute. Then another and another until Kate finally gasped, "It stopped!"

Her uncle nodded cautiously but said nothing.

Slowly, a thought came to her mind. "Maybe," she said out loud, "maybe there's nothing to eat here. It's just rock. Maybe."

They waited. Kate, for the first time, noticed the smell, the moist, acrid stench of the fungus. It nearly gagged her. Then she realized she was hot, very hot. She was unsure but thought top layer of slime was beginning to retreat. She felt herself falling. She felt her uncle grab her.

17

A fire in her throat brought Kate back to consciousness. Her head wheeled and she could barely move her legs. Her eyes slowly focused on the water bottles and the cans of food goods and then the floor and then the steps. She looked around but Andrew was gone.

She sat up and had to wait for the room to stop spinning. Focusing on the steps, she saw that the slime had changed. It was no longer black. It was no longer frozen. It was gray. And it no longer moved. It looked like concrete. Moving forward cautiously, she prodded the slime with her foot and it cracked and flaked into a fine gray powder. Then she noticed the footprints leading up the steps. She followed her uncle's footprints into the brilliance of a new day.

The sky was bright blue and billowy with clouds. She had to shield her eyes from the sun as she looked around. The refrigerator stood upright in a sea of brittle gray concrete. The stove was still there, as was the stone fireplace, naked under the sun.

Andrew was standing where his front porch used to be. He was looking at the sea, at the shimmering, pale water that ran wide and beautiful before him, as if the black death had never come. Kate crunched her way over the dead slime to stand next to him. She tucked her arm into his, gently. She could not control the smile that engulfed her face as she watched the sea.

"I watched it break up on the waves and sink," he told her. He moved his foot forward and crunched more of the decayed slime into powder. "The wind will take it all away," he added.

And, as if it heard him, a breath of sea breeze flowed over them and blew the broken flakes away to reveal the stone surface of the island.

Kate turned around and looked at the mainland, at the gray desolation as far as she could see.

"The whole world's gone," she said.

"No it isn't. The slime never crosses the Perfume Mountains. Everyone's still safe in the cities."

"Are you sure?"

Her uncle pointed to the west, to the mountains in the distance. He handed Kate the binoculars. She could see the mountains were still green.

"It's the legend," he said as he put his arm around her shoulder.

"But your house?"

He surprised her by laughing. "Hell," he said, "guess I'll just have to build another one. After all, I'm only sixty. And the damn slime won't be back for another hundred years."

The legend again, she told herself. She looked back at the sea. In the distance, off to her right, she saw three pterodactyls flapping their way out over the water.

Her uncle looked up and laughed at the pesky bastards.

THE END *of*
"Slimy Things Did Crawl Upon The Slimy Sea"

It Rumbled

Under the water it rumbled on,
Still louder and more dread:
It reached the ship, it split the bay;
The ship went down like lead.

> "The Rime of the Ancient Mariner"
> Samuel Taylor Coleridge (Earth, 1798 a.d.)

One of those pterodactyl things landed on a boulder above where we lay and whistled loudly. Its whistle was answered immediately by others I couldn't see. My son twitched in his sleep and pressed his little body against me. The pterodactyl spread its leathery wings and jumped off the boulder, flapped twice before folding its wings and diving over us down into the sea. I could see it in the dim dawn light, as it rose from the water, a large black crustacean in its beak. It swooped to my right and disappeared from sight behind the high rocks.

I lay still as Vincent twitched again. Curled in a fetal position, his arms tucked against his chest, his hands were drawn into little fists. I looked at his face, at the tiny hairs along the side of his face where sideburns would grow when he grew up. I brushed his straight, dark brown hair away from his eyes. His mouth pursed, he looked so much like his mother.

I repositioned myself and closed my eyes. I felt him twitch again, and then his young voice cried out, "Icky, Icky, Daddy. Icky!"

I wrapped my arm around him and hugged him and said, "Vincent, wake up. You're dreaming."

His wide, brown eyes batted at me and his lips quivered as he said, "Daddy, I felt it. The boat shaked."

"I know son, but we're on land now. It can't hurt us."

Vincent raised his head, blinked and then buried his face against my shoulder and snuggled with me. "The boat rumbled, Daddy."

"I know, son. But it was just a dream. Go back to sleep."

I couldn't sleep. No way. That same dream woke me hours earlier. Sure, we were safe now, a good fifty yards from the ichthyosaurs that cruised the Cobalt Sea with their lifeless black eyes and wide jaws and yellow saber teeth. But we weren't safe from the dreams, from the memory of how the big creatures attacked our boat, how the boat shuddered as they rolled beneath it, tearing it apart, sending us into the sea.

Vincent tumbled into the water and I dove in after him. I found him in the warm, clear water, pulled him up as an Ichthyosaurus glided past, its green fin pushing us up to the surface. The sharp, salt water burned my throat. Vincent coughed and wrapped his arms around my neck and his legs around my waist and I swam and swam, the strong Octavion sun beating down on us, transforming the turquoise water into silver. I felt the swell of water as an Icky closed in. And I swam harder.

I don't remember the rest. I woke on the beach with Vincent patting my head, his face half-covered with sand. I pulled him close and hugged him so hard he started laughing and said I was giving him *squeezy-wheezies* again.

Now on our twenty-first day on the island, I rose and stretched in the early morning light. I reached down and grabbed the sail of pterodactyl wings I was making for our raft and draped it over my son. Then I felt the ground shiver beneath my feet. And Vincent cried out again.

"It rumbled, Daddy!"

He looked up at me with sleepy eyes and then glanced around. The ground shook again, and he sat up and spread his hands out on the ground.

"It's just the mountain," I said, looking up the sheer rise of the rust brown mountain as a distant gray cloud belched from its summit. I smelled the thick sulfur fumes. Turning, I looked out at the Cobalt Sea just as the sun peeked up over the horizon, shining gold on the pale blue water.

Our fire was nearly out, so I put more driftwood on it and stoked it until it flared up.

"I'm hungry," Vincent said behind me. He rearranged his shirt which had twisted around in his sleep.

"Well, let's get something to eat." I picked up my bow and strung it, carefully checking the gut string. The driftwood bow bent nicely as I pulled back on the gut.

"String's still good?" Vincent asked.

"Sure."

The gut was from the first pterodactyl I'd killed, clubbing it to death for our first fresh meat, when was that, the sixth day?

Vincent picked up his small spear and handed me my larger one. I slipped the stainless steel folding knife into the pocket of my pants and grabbed a handful of stone-tipped, fire-hardened arrows and said, "Okay, let's go."

"First we gotta pee."

Climbing off the rocks, Vincent lead the way down to the small beach were we peed in the sea. I watched the sun creep higher, like a golden disk rising from the water.

"I'm gonna beat you," Vincent said as he zipped up his pants and hurried to the first tide pool.

"Slow down," I said, scanning the sky for the pesky pterodactyls. Too small to attack me, I still wasn't sure if they'd attack my boy.

Vincent bounced back over the rocks to the first tide pool and peeked over in it. He turned his face back to me and put a finger over his mouth.

"Shhh," he whispered. "Lobsters!"

The ground felt warmer beneath my bare feet next to the first tide pool. I peeked over. Two large lobsters and a smaller one glided in the green, crystal water.

I eased the tip of my spear into the pool and waited until the largest lobster moved under it. I drove the tip down hard and felt it sink into the lobster. With a wide swing, I flung the lobster over my shoulder onto the rocks. It flapped wildly.

I let it lay a moment and watched Vincent try to spear the smaller lobster. His spear struck, but didn't go in and the lobster scurried away.

"Damn," Vincent said as he lunged his spear at the other large lobster, which dove deep and slipped away through the vent back into the sea.

I grabbed Vincent around the waist and pulled him away from the edge. "Don't fall in."

"Daddy!" Vincent wiggled away. "I'm not dumb."

At seven he was a handful. Hell, he'd always been quite a handful.

"Come on." I walked over and pulled the large lobster from my spear. We walked back across the rocks, around the steam geysers to the fire. I handed Vincent the largest pterodactyl skull and told him to get some fresh water.

I pretended not to watch but kept a careful eye as he climbed the rocks up to the large spring above us where the water was always warm, but fresh at least. I wrapped the lobster between two branches and moved over to a steam vent and steamed it. When Vincent stepped up, I handed him the branches.

"Just hold it there." I walked over to another tide pool and speared another lobster, even bigger.

"Wow," Vincent said, lifting his left hand over his eyes to shield them from the sun. I wrapped the second lobster in branches and sat next to my son and steamed it. It didn't take long for both to turn deep red.

Vincent reached over with his free hand and ran his fingers across the sharp tips of my arrows. He smiled at me and said, "You know how many arrows it takes to kills a Tyrannosaurus rex?"

"No."

"Ninety."

I nodded.

"Or fifty-nine."

Where he came with stuff like that was beyond me. I don't remember being that precocious when I was a kid. Then again, on Earth the only tyrannosaurs we had were toys.

"You know what I'd do if there was a Tyrannosaurus on this island?" he asked.

"No."

"I'd punch him in the balls."

I put my hand on the top of his head and turned his face to me. "Balls? Where did you learn that?"

"School." He grinned up at me and then wiggled back a few inches away from the steam.

His mother would be proud of the language he was picking up at St. George's School. "It's the best in Silver City," she'd said. "One of the best on all of Octavion." That was right after the divorce. I'd agreed.

I thought about her a moment, as we steamed our lobsters. She was probably hotter than the lobsters by now. I was supposed to have Vincent for two weeks. The Ickys sure wrecked havoc with our visitation schedule.

"Let's bathe while they cool off," I said when we pulled our crimson lobsters from the steam. I picked up my bow and arrows and led the way over to the large warm spring on the other side of the boulders where we stripped down, climbed in and soaked.

I reached back and pulled the knife out of my pants before dunking my shirt and pants in the water. I pulled Vincent's white cotton shirt that was no longer white, and his brown shorts into the warm water too. I washed the clothes as best I could before laying them on a sunny rock next to the pool.

Settling back in the water, I saw how Vincent's olive complexion had grown so dark from the sun. His butt was like a streak of whitewash. I'm sure I was just as dark, if not darker.

"Wanna go see if your gun washed up on the beach yet?"

I looked back at my son as he mimicked my position now, his arms up along the rocks, his body straight out in the water.

"It's at the bottom of the sea," I said.

"The knife washed up, didn't it?"

I nodded. The day after I clubbed my first pterodactyl we found the stainless steel folding knife on the beach. My rifle had been in the boat's cabin. It was at the bottom of the sea.

I closed my eyes a moment and faced the bright sun. Perspiration worked its way out on my face, and I dunked under and then climbed out of the water.

Our clothes were already dry.

We cracked open the lobsters and feasted on the sweet white meat, washing it down with the warm, spring water from the pterodactyl skull. Then we went to work on the raft.

There was plenty of driftwood on the beaches, especially on the long beach where we landed three weeks ago. Using vines from the bushes, I'd managed to tie enough driftwood together into a crude raft. One straight piece of wood would serve as a mast for the pterodactyl-wing sail. Another short one would make a perfect boom.

Vincent helped by holding the wood together while I tied each piece to the raft. After attaching all the pieces we collected yesterday, we walked along the sand. Vincent used his spear to chase fiddler crabs, while I slung my bow over my shoulder and carried my arrows, keeping a wary eye on the sky.

Vincent stopped and turned to the sea and shielded his eyes with his hands. "How do you know it's only fifteen miles away?"

He pointed his spear toward the mainland, toward the Calico Hills within easy sight of the island. So close and yet so far. Too far to swim. I shielded my eyes and looked across the azure water. Off to our right a swarm of pterodactyls glided on the air currents. One closed its wings and plunged into the crystalline water. It rose a moment later, and another fell into the sea.

Looking back toward the mainland, I spotted two large dark objects under the waves. One broke the surface, its dorsal fin rolling forward as the ichthyosaur took a whiff of air before diving again.

Vincent stood stiffly now, his big eyes following the movement of the monsters in the clear water. Slowly, he inched away from the water and bumped into me.

"Are they looking for more boats?"

"No. They're coming up for air."

"They don't breathe under water?"

I wished I could tell him they were like whales, only there were no whales on Octavion. "No, son. They breathe air. Like us."

We found six long pieces of driftwood and dragged them back to the raft. We sat in the sand, next to our raft and tied them, the sun bringing perspiration to our faces and arms. The mountain rumbled again. Then an explosion rocked the ground. I looked up and saw a streak of red at the top of the mountain.

"Vincent." I lifted the raft.

"Get under!" I climbed in after him. Three heartbeats later, the rocks peppered us almost a minute. Vincent grabbed my leg and squeezed. A breath of stale, sulfuric steam covered us for a moment but blew away just as quickly. I peeked out and looked up at the sky. A long stream of black rose straight up as far as I could see.

"Is lava going to get us?" Vincent poked his face out from under my arm.

"No. Not yet."

I didn't tell him that's why we had to hurry with the raft. He knew.

On our way to gather more driftwood, Vincent kicked at two large black rocks that sat steaming on the beach. He reached down and touched one of the smaller rocks, but pulled back immediately.

"It's hot," he said.

I found two larger pieces of driftwood and started dragging them back when one of those pterodactyls landed on the low branch of a dead tree not twenty feet from us. Jerking its head around like a bird, it looked at Vincent and started the whistling sound again.

I heard another answer behind me as I put the driftwood down, pulled my bow off and strung an arrow. I pulled back and aimed and let it fly. The arrow's stone tip smacked into the pterodactyl just below its neck. It squealed and opened its wings and leapt into the air. It flapped once, then sputtered and fell headlong on the beach. I reached it quickly, pinning its head down with the bow. Then I pulled out the folding knife and stopped its squealing. Leaning back on my haunches I felt Vincent's hand on my shoulder as I looked up at three more pterodactyls circling and whistling.

"That's the biggest yet," Vincent said, leaning around me to get a good look at the dead beast. He was right. This one was nearly twenty pounds. The others had been under ten.

I re-slung the bow around me, wiped the knife off on the belly of the pterodactyl and refolded the knife before slipping it back into my pocket. I picked the beast up by its feet and went back for the driftwood.

As the sun fell behind the rust mountain, casting its long shadow across us, we finished the raft. I wove the new pterodactyl wings to the bottom of the sail and strung the sail to the mast and the boom.

"You see," I told Vincent. "All I have to do is set the mast here in this hole and if there's a wind, the sail will take us to the mainland."

"What if the wind's blowing the other way?"

I scooped up some sand and tossed it in the air. It blew toward the mainland.

"Have I ever told you about prevailing winds?"

"Are you joking me again?"

• • •

Before dark, we each grabbed two pterodactyl skulls and went up to get fresh water. On our way back from the spring, we spotted a gray ground squirrel eating red berries from some bramble bushes. We stopped and picked the bushes clean to go with our pterodactyl steaks for supper.

"Don't go far," I told Vincent as I roasted two thick steaks over the fire.

I watched my boy play with three fiddler crabs as the steaks cooked. I felt two more rumbles from the mountain before the steaks were done. I poured water over the large flat boulder we'd been using as a table and cut both steaks up with the folding knife before calling Vincent over.

"Wash your hands."

As usual, the steak was chewy, but tasted delicious. Vincent downed two pieces quickly, before I had to tell him to chew it well. He grinned at me, meat between his teeth, and said, "I know. I know."

The berries were tangy and went very well with the meat.

Finishing off the last of the steak, I saw Vincent sit up stiffly, staring over my shoulder. I turned and looked at the semi-darkness.

"What is it?"

"I think I saw a Velociraptor." He pointed to three large boulders behind me.

I stood up and grabbed the knife, as if it would do any good against a raptor.

"You sure?"

"I . . . I think so."

I switched the knife to my left hand and picked up one of my spears. I narrowed my eyes and listened as hard as I could, but only heard the faint rumble of the volcano and the roll of the waves behind us. I dropped the spear and reached into the fire and pulled out a burning stick and moved Vincent behind me. Back on Earth, I remembered, wild animals were afraid of fire.

"You're not joking me, are you son?"

"No, Daddy." He shook his head.

After a long minute, I stoked the fire and tossed more driftwood on it until it raged. Then Vincent and I sat next to it and studied the darkness around us.

"Don't worry, Daddy." I felt Vincent's hand on my arm. "My hands are like lightning. I'll kick its butt."

The sound of the sea increased at night. The mountain's rumbling died down until it sounded like a giant's belly growling from hunger. Vincent sat with his back pressed against my side. I switched fiery sticks, keeping a fresh one in my left hand, the knife in my right hand.

"Know what you'd have if you mixed a Tyrannosaurus rex and a Velociraptor?"

"No." I looked down at his little face.

"Dead raptor." He said it deadpan, then grinned up at me with a grin so wide, his eyes were slits.

I kept telling myself if there were raptors on the island, they would have found us long ago, even if the island was big enough that it took us two days to walk around it. Then again, maybe the volcano had driven the raptors our way.

Finally, I felt my shoulders relax from the tension of straining to see or hear anything beyond what our fire illuminated. I lined three nice pieces of wood at the edge of the fire, pieces I could use as a torch to swing. As if that would do any good.

Octavion, this beautiful planet of primeval forests and crystal seas, of brightly colored hills and wondrous waterfalls, held a great mystery of the galaxy. It was a dinosaur planet, inhabited by pterodactyl-like creatures, raptors and even mighty tyrannosaurs. The greatest scientific minds don't know why, had come up with no scientific explanation. It was as nebulous as the great attraction that drew us humans here. Someone once said it was a search for Earth's past beauty.

I fed the fire until it raged, then went and picked up my three straightest spears and sharpened them next to the fire, rubbing them on the hot rocks until they were as pointy as a needle. Vincent stretched out and put his head on my knee, using it as a pillow. I watched the fire light dance over his young face. He was growing up so fast. I could still remember him toddling down the hall of our old house to tap me on the shoulder so he could climb in bed with us and clamber up on my belly to sleep. I could still hear his two-year-old high-low voice that wasn't used to pitch yet as he'd say, "Daddy. Get hugs Vincent, Daddy."

I felt a well of emotion tighten my throat as I looked down at my boy. I'd worried so much about how he would handle my leaving, growing up in a broken home. I just never figured how much I'd lose, how painful it would be for me not being with him every day like this.

I reached over and touched his arm. I missed touching him every night, missed his hugs, his eager eyes batting at me when he asked me questions. He once asked me why I moved out. I told him that his mother and I just couldn't live together anymore. We just didn't get along. He said he understood, but I could see, in his deep brown eyes that he didn't.

I looked down at Vincent again and wished, with all my heart, that he and I could stay together forever. At least until he grew up. I did not want to miss his young years. In some sort of macabre response, the volcano trembled again above us.

So I sat out the night feeding the fire, my son curled next to me as I searched the darkness for killers that could strike so silently, the only sound you would hear would be your body striking the ground. The mountain started up again, helping me to stay awake with its growling.

When morning finally came, a wide streak of sky was stained black with ash from the volcano. Vincent batted his eyes up at it and said, "Did I miss something?"

I smiled at him. "I chased off two raptors last night."

"You're joking me. I know it."

The breeze tousled my hair as I stood up and stretched. He stood and stretched too.

"Ready to take a ride on the raft?"

"Really?"

I put a couple pterodactyl steaks on sticks and roasted them over the fire for breakfast while we filled the pterodactyl skulls with water from the stream. Then we went and checked the raft. On the way back Vincent stepped away from me and pointed to the sand. "Daddy. Look."

There was a trail of footprints in the wet sand.

"Raptor." Vincent bent over and touched the edge of one of the prints.

I'm not sure what a Velociraptor's footprint looks like, but whatever made these prints was bigger than me. The prints had circled the fire.

"Let's eat by the raft," I said.

87

• • •

"Sit here." I pointed to a hollow in the piece of driftwood than ran down the center of the raft. Vincent's butt was small enough to fit in the hollow and he could use the broken branch behind as a back rest.

"What are you doing?" he asked when I tied the vines around his waist. I told him it was like a seatbelt.

"Hold on tight, son."

I climbed off and pushed the raft into the water. I waited until a small wave broke to shore and followed it out into the surf, pushing the raft as long as I could reach bottom with my feet. Then I swam behind it, kicking my legs hard until we eased out of the surf into the calm sea.

"Daddy."

"What?"

Vincent looked back at the beach. "Raptors can't swim, can they?"

I looked back but didn't see anything on the beach.

"You saw something?"

"I joked you. I joked you!"

I felt something brush against my legs and climbed aboard quickly. I looked over but saw nothing in the clear water, except seaweed. Standing, I moved to the center of the raft and hoisted the mast with its pterodactyl sail. The wind caught it immediately and the raft lurched forward. I hurried back, holding the vine attached to the boom, and sat behind Vincent.

"What's that?" he said when I hooked the crude rudder over the back of the raft.

"It's what steers the raft."

A brisk wind filled the sail and the raft moved quickly over the smooth water of the Cobalt Sea.

"Wheee!" Vincent opened his arms.

I looked around without him seeing me look around. The sun glittered off the water to my right. The turquoise water was streaked with patches of purple and dark blue off to my left. I could see clearly for a long way, and there were no dark shapes.

A pop behind us turned both our heads around. Two red swatches of lava rolled down the top of the mountain now, in long stains. Maybe, just maybe the volcanic activity would keep the ichthyosaurs away, I told myself. When I was a boy, we called that wishful thinking. At the university they called it the power of positive thinking. I held on to the vine holding the boom and to the rudder and sailed straight for the mainland.

The air felt cooler over the water. An occasional splash of salty water washed over us. A fine mist bathed my face, leaving a saline taste on my lips. We made good time. The miles slipped behind us, and we closed slowly and steadily on the mainland.

Vincent turned back to look at me and grinned, then looked out at the water, shielding his eyes from the sun with his hands. Every so often, he'd looked back at me and raise his eyebrows or just grin. His sun-darkened face turned pale when we felt a shudder beneath the raft.

I glanced to my left and saw it, the bright-green dorsal fin roll out from beneath us, the long stain of its body sliding down into the blue water. The Ichthyosaurus rolled deeper and moved away from us. The raft settled in the water and bumped forward on the light waves.

I looked at the mainland. We were still miles from it. I could see a white beach now and a tree line behind it. The Calico Hills rose from the beach like a distant heaven so far from our reach. When I looked back at Vincent, his eyes stared at me widely.

"It's all right son. It's gone now."

Slowly he looked out at the water. He bit his lower lip, and I could see his little chest rise and fall. I wrapped the boom vine around my left arm and switched my left hand to the rudder so I could reach the four spears I had sharpened last night. I pulled them close to me.

Cupping a spear in my right hand, I looked around at the sea, at the quiet water, but there was no dark stain. I had to squint to look to my right with the sun dancing on the water. The bastard had come from the sun on its first pass. It would probably come that way again.

I looked up at the beach for a second, wishing I could reach out and yank us to it. The movement of Vincent's head pulled my gaze back. He looked from side to side now, back and forth, his hair dancing in the breeze. The raft took a lurch forward in a sudden gust of wind, and Vincent's head stopped moving as he stared to our right. I looked over just in time to see the fin rise from the water and strike the raft, spinning us half way around.

Vincent screamed. I held on, moving the boom around to catch the wind, as the Icky lumbered past. Its back was scarred with white barnacles. I heard it suck in a deep breath of air before sinking.

It took a long minute to maneuver the raft back around toward the mainland. Vincent stopped screaming. He looked at me with his lower lip shaking. I was about to tell him it was gone, when I saw it again, ahead and off to our left. It rolled in the water, its triangular side fin rising now, its head twisting up in the air. Its huge jaws opened, yellow teeth gliding past as the swell of its body pushed us hard to the right. Its jaws were as long as the raft.

Vincent watched it pass, his mouth opened in a wide "O," his shoulders slumped.

Climbing up on my knees, I re-wrapped the sail vine around my left arm, still holding the rudder with the same hand. I raised my spear to my shoulder with my right hand. I watched the Icky move around us.

It maneuvered ahead of us again and came at us head on. I pushed the rudder away from me and we veered to the right. The dorsal fin rolled down and the tip of its huge jaws broke the surface, snapping, cascading water over us as it passed.

I raised the spear and threw it. The tip struck the side of the Icky's jaw and bounced off as it rolled by. Its swell propelled us forward, and I could feel the beach reaching for us. I wiped the water from my eyes and the beach grew closer. I could make out individual trees now.

"Daddy! Daddy!"

The Icky rose from the water off to our right and leaped into the air, nearly its entire huge body suspended in the air for a moment before it twisted to the right, snapped its hideous jaw and slapped back into the sea.

"Hold on!" I yelled as the giant wave lifted us and shoved us hard to the left. I held on to the sail, my left arm aching with the pull of the sail and trying to hold the rudder.

As soon as we settled, I picked up another spear.

"Over there!" Vincent pointed to the left now. The Icky moved away from us. It was then I spotted another dorsal fin off to the left as another approached. I looked at the long line of white beach much closer now.

"Where is it?" Vincent bounced as he sat, looking around.

"I don't know." My left arm throbbed with the pain, but I kept the sail to the wind and we continued forward so slowly it was painful.

The Icky surfaced off to our left and headed straight for us. I saw my son bury his chin against his chest and look away. I rose on my knees and raised my spear high. The Icky opened its hideous jaws and snapped them shut and slipped to the left slightly. I jerked the rudder to my right and we twisted in the wind.

The head came out of the water again, and I saw its black eye as it rolled next to us. I threw the spear with all my might and saw it strike just below the lifeless eye. It stuck. And the Icky sank with it into the water.

We rode the swell again. I struggled to right us, watching the Icky as it turned and came for us again. When it broke the surface I saw the spear still sticking out of it. I grabbed another spear as it came from behind us. I threw the spear at the other eye, but it struck the edge of its jaw and bounced away. I spotted the other Icky now, off in the distance. It was pacing us.

Vincent was silent now, his head pressed back against the branch, his eyes closed. I reached forward and touched his face, and he opened his eyes and looked at me and tried to smile.

We inched closer to the beach with each heartbeat.

My left arm was numb from pain.

I grabbed my last spear as the Icky came at us again head on.

Pulling the rudder around hard, I tried to get out of its way, but it moved with us and sank beneath the surface. I felt my heartbeat thundering in my ears now as the raft stopped dead in the water for a moment.

Vincent looked at me, his dark eyes wide and suddenly unafraid as if this was our last look. I felt my throat catch as the front of the raft rose and the water fell away below us. The raft rolled up and then we fell hard into the sea, the warm water grabbing us and pulling us down. We spun beneath the water and then broke the surface, and I reached for Vincent. His head was forward and limp. I lunged for him and felt the Icky strike the raft, heard the snap of the driftwood as the raft collapsed.

I pulled out my knife, cut my left arm free and cut the vines that held Vincent and pulled him to me. His eyes opened and he smiled at me and coughed out a faint, "Daddy." We sank into the water together. I dropped the knife and pulled my son on my back. He wrapped his arms around my neck as we broke the surface. We both coughed. I told him to wrap his legs around my back, and I shoved away from the broken raft.

And I swam for the beach. I swam in long, smooth strokes, kicking my legs and pulling with my arms, keeping both of our heads out of the salty water.

Another loud noise snapped behind us.

"He ate the raft, Daddy."

I bore down straight for the beach.

Vincent's hands tightened around my neck, and I remembered the first time I saw my son, remembered the doctor passing him to me after they'd cleaned him off, remembered his wide eyes looking up at me as if he was saying, "Well, I'm here, Daddy. What are you going to do with me?"

It was the greatest moment in my life.

And now, as I struggled with the sea, as we struggled toward the beach, I felt a peaceful feeling when he squeezed my neck. We were together. No matter what happened to us now, we were together, my son and me. I felt my muscles ease and felt us moving quicker in the water with longer strokes now.

I stroked again and again and again, pulling at the water, kicking my legs and it was as if I were in a trance – my arms, my legs, the water, the sun, my son. Until I felt a wave swell behind and shove us forward and felt my right hand hit something solid beneath me.

I opened my eyes and squinted at the bright, white sand of the beach.

I felt Vincent climb off and try to pull me up. I crawled out of the water up on hot sand and collapsed. I felt my son patting my hair. I reached around and pulled him close and hugged his waist.

When I looked up, he grinned at me.

It took a while before I could get up and move us off the steamy sand to the shade of a palm tree at the edge of the woods. Vincent sat next to me, his back, like mine, pressed against the tree trunk.

I'm not sure how much time passed before we heard something in the woods behind us. I turned and saw the bright blue uniform of a Coast Guardsman moving right for us. Well tanned, with white blond hair, the guardsman called out to us. "You people all right?"

I managed to nod. Vincent got up and moved around me to sit on my left side, staring at the guardsman as the man stepped up.

The man folded his arms and said, "You didn't go swimming out there, did you?"

Gasping, I struggled with my parched throat. "Where? Where . . . did . . . you . . . come from?"

"Down the beach," he said. Pointing back over his shoulder. "We've been searching for survivors. A boat wend down around here yesterday? You from it?"

I shook my head. "Another boat." I pointed to the island and the plume of smoke rising, managed to say, "Marooned."

Vincent leaned his head back against my shoulder and looked at me.

"You shouldn't swim out there," the guardsman said. "It's full of ichthyosaurs."

Vincent shielded his eyes and looked up at the man. "We know that, you big dummy." Turning his beaming face to me, my son said, "That sure was a close one, huh Dad?"

THE END *of* "It Rumbled"

for my son Vincent

Happy Living Things

O happy living things! no tongue
Their beauty might declare …
A spring of love gushed from my heart,
And I blessed them unaware

> "The Rime of the Ancient Mariner"
> Samuel Taylor Coleridge (Earth, 1798 a.d.)

Along the backwash of the Milky Way hovered a sun-kissed planet of painted oceans and brightly-colored seas with names such as the Cobalt Sea, the Cerulean Sea and the Sapphire Sea and rivers called Majestic Blue and Royal Blue. Planet Octavion featured great plateaus, the Copper Plateau and the Terra Cotta Plateau and the multi-colored Calico Hills and Cinnamon Hills, the orange-brown color of cinnamon.

Forests covered much of the planet and were named for the colors of their trees – the Magenta Forest with pinkish-purple trees and the Spearmint Forest of bright green tree trunks, the vast Indigo Forest of dark blue trees with pale blue leaves. The stone beneath Lake Violet gave its water a purplish cast and the green limestone of Emerald Lake gave its water a deep green color.

When the humans came to Octavion, riding the wave of the Right of Habitation Act, giving people the right to colonize any inhabitable world, they were amazed by the bright colors, like children in a toy store, naming the forests and rivers for their vivid colors.

They also brought their machines and computers and the inevitable clash of worlds began immediately, native species edged aside by Earth creatures – cows and chickens and horses and cats and dogs.

After thirty years and a million human inhabitants, the Indigenous Creature Act was passed to protect native species, giving them the right of way in most instances. One summer evening, as the huge Octavion sun hung just above the horizon, a girl named Dana learned the great lesson of The Indigenous Creature Act.

Sitting on a green-wood bench beneath a towering spearmint tree, Dana spied a movement beyond the low stone wall at the rear of the school yard. Something stepped up from the Charcoal Plain. The waning sunlight glimmered on its silver horn, its golden mane flowing in the warm breeze. It was so white it was hard to see, even in the twilight but Dana knew it was a unicorn and her heart began to beat furiously. The unicorn poked its snout over the wall and nibbled the coral leaves of the large burgundy bush just inside the yard.

Dana sat frozen, afraid to even blink, and watched the most beautiful of creatures as it ate the leaves. It ate every leaf it could reach before turning slowing and moving away. Crouching, Dana hurried to the low wall and watched the unicorn disappear into the ever-increasing darkness.

The bell rang behind Dana. Suppertime at Mrs. Miniver's Private Summer Camp for Girls. The other girls would be hurrying to the dining room. Dana was last to arrive, her heart still thumping with her secret safely inside. Tomorrow, she thought. She'd gather as many coral leaves as she could and pile them atop the wall and wait.

"Where have you been?" her new friend Joanie asked when Dana plopped her tray on the table.

"Reading," Dana answered, knowing Joanie wouldn't ask any more. Reading at summer camp? What was the fun in that? Both girls were twelve, Dana with dark brown hair and bright green eyes, Joanie with blonde hair and brown eyes, much fairer.

In bed that evening, Dana closed her eyes and day-dreamed about the unicorn as it raced between the dark gray rocks of the Charcoal Plain, rearing on its hind legs, snorting, then scratching the ground with its front hooves before stepping over to let Dana pet it.

The girls went swimming the next day at the shallow end of Lake Robin whose pale blue water matched the color of a robin's egg. Dana had never seen a robin's egg, nor a robin from that matter.

Like her big brother Vincent, Dana was born on Octavion. Her Mom and Dad were Earthlings, as they called themselves, especially when they told the kids how special it was to be born on a planet without all the problems and pollution. Like most native Octavions, there were many Earth things Dana had only seen in pictures, like unicorns, until the previous evening. But it wasn't even a picture of a unicorn she'd seen before, it was a drawing.

"There are no unicorns," Mrs. Miniver told Dana when she asked, as casually as she could. "There never were, not even on Earth." Mrs. Miniver sat in the water, her gray hair up in a bun atop her head. "They were mythical creatures, like mermaids and fairies."

Joanie splashed water on two other girls, who screeched. Dana closed her eyes to envision mythical creatures, mermaids and unicorns splashing together in the shallow water of the lake. A spray of water in the face, from a giggling Joanie, brought Dana back to the present.

That evening Dana was surprised when Joanie caught her dotting the rear wall with coral leaves just before suppertime and asked, "What are you doing?"

Dana looked around guiltily and tried to think of something to fool her friend, but there was no way Joanie would just leave and the unicorn might come any time. So Dana led Joanie to the green-wood bench and told her to wait and see.

"Can you keep a secret?"

Joanie said she could.

"I'm serious," Dana said.

Joanie nodded. When she asked, "What are we waiting for?" Dana shushed her.

As the sun was about to set, Dana spotted the gleam of silver and the golden mane as the unicorn came out of the dimness to nibble the leaves she'd sprinkled atop the wall.

Joanie let out a long breath and Dana shushed her again as the unicorn ate the leaves. Noises behind the girls, some of the girls horsing around, caused the unicorn's head to lift twice, but it kept moving along the wall, eating. Dana didn't see the second unicorn until she heard it whinny and step up to the wall and join the first, nibbling the coral leaves. Joanie grabbed Dana's arm and squeezed and Dana opened her eyes wide in alarm, hoping Joanie would keep quiet. The second unicorn was slightly smaller than the first and Dana thought it was a girl, a filly and the first, a stallion.

The unicorns ate all the leaves, then turned and moved away. Dana, crouched again, ran to the wall with Joanie right behind and watched the smaller unicorn nuzzle the bigger one as they disappeared into the gathering darkness.

After supper, the girls returned to the back yard and gathered more coral leaves, piling in the far corner for the next day. They sat back on the bench. Dana felt sad and it must have shown on her face, because Joanie asked what was wrong.

"They are so beautiful," said Dana.

"Why … why is that sad?"

"Because someone will want to catch them, might even hurt them."

"Why would they do that?" Joanie's voice caught. Dana could see the fear in her friend's eyes now.

"Maybe, just maybe that's what happened to unicorns on Earth."

Joanie nodded slowly. "But I heard Mrs. Miniver say there weren't any unicorns on Earth. Ever."

So she *had* been listening.

"But they're here, aren't they?" Dana said.

"But what can we do about it?"

Dana thought, if only she could talk to her father. He had given an emergency contact number to Mrs. Miniver. He was out "in the field" as he put it, not at his office or at home. But Mrs. Miniver would want to know what was the emergency.

"You know," Dana said after a few minutes of silence. "These might be the last unicorns in the universe." She felt the hair standing up on the back of her neck and a sudden chill.

• • •

At breakfast the following morning, Dana felt nervous and frustrated. Her father would know exactly what to do about the unicorns and if she could keep anyone else from finding out about them until then, then everything might be OK. But she had to do *something*.

A plan began to form in Dana's mind and she worked on it all day. She loved animals, especially baby animals. She imagined what a unicorn colt must look like, with its tiny horn. The more she thought about it, the more she was convinced she *had* to do something.

"We're going to follow them," she told Joanie that evening as they spread the leaves atop the wall.

"Follow them? Out there?"

Dana pointed to the knapsack she'd hidden behind one of the burgundy bushes.

"They must live close by," Dana said. "I've got flashlights and water bottles and food." Then she explained that if they could show her father where the unicorns lived, then it would be easy to protect them.

"Can he really protect them?"

"That's what he does," Dana said with pride.

The unicorns came early that evening and Dana worried someone else might see them, but the teachers were busy with the girls, most rehearsing for the school play or bouncing basketballs in the gym. Some, like Dana, would be expected to be in the library or like Joanie, who usually stayed in the rec room watching movies.

The filly came first with the stallion right behind and they nibbled the leaves as casually as if the leaves grew naturally atop the wall. Dana found she was holding her breath as she turned her head around slowly to make sure no one else was watching.

When the unicorns moved away, Dana led Joanie to the knapsack and the girls easily climbed over the wall and started after the unicorns. Both girls wore long pants and long-sleeved shirts for the impending night and hiking boots, instead of the usual sneakers worn at summer camp.

Crossing the wide Charcoal Plain with its dark gray rocks and occasional patches of aqua-colored grass, they moved directly for the nearby Cranberry Hills. The unicorns moved at a leisurely pace twisting around the rocks and occasional boulders. Their trail wound its way toward the hills.

Darkness enveloped them as they neared the first hill, its dark red color seeming almost black now. They could still see the shining white unicorns and followed them through the creepy darkness. It became so black, even the ground disappeared. A high-pitched yipping made Dana jump. A scraping sound behind them, turned Dana around. Sudden footfalls made her heart leap and Joanie grab her hand.

"What's that?" Joanie whispered and Dana heard a low growling, followed by more footfalls. She looked back at the unicorns that were still moving away, so she pulled Joanie along. Joanie tripped over a rock and almost fell, Dana helped her up and when she looked back, she saw the unicorns walk straight into the side of a hill.

"Where'd they go?" Joanie asked.

Dana took a hesitant step forward, reached into the knapsack and pulled out the flashlights, passing one to Joanie. It was even more eerie with the flashlights on, the blackness seemed even darker around them and there were more sounds now, yipping and hurried footfalls.

It took them ten minutes of frightful searching to find the entrance to the cave.

"I don't want to go in there," Joanie said.

"Then stay out here by yourself." Dana stepped into the wide mouth of the cave and shined her light around the dark red walls. She felt her knees shaking and knew she was afraid but she didn't want Joanie to know so she clenched her teeth to keep them from chattering and continued into the cave. Joanie followed.

Swinging her flashlight around, she could see the cave was so wide, the beam barely reached the sides and the ceiling. Something small scurried past, making Dana jump and Joanie screech.

"Whatever it was, it was small." Dana said.

"It could have been a snake."

"There are no snakes on Octavion."

"There aren't supposed to be any unicorns *either.*"

Dana had to admit, Joanie had a good point, so she paid more attention to the floor as they inched forward. Dana didn't realize she was hearing something until the sound increased. Running water. The girls stopped and swung their beams around but there was no water. It took a few moments to decide the sound came from in front of them.

The cave made a turn to the right and suddenly it was completely black in front of them. Their beams fell away into darkness and Dana focused on the floor again and saw the edge of the cave falling away in a steep decline.

The sound of water was louder now, running water, a stream or a river just below them.

"What do we do now?" Joanie's voice broke.

"We wait until morning."

"All night? In here?"

"Do we have a choice?" Dana moved to the side of the cave and dropped the knapsack, reaching inside for the fire log and the lighter. "Do you want to go back across the plain? At night?"

Joanie shook her head.

"This lasts eight hours." Dana pointed to the log as she assembled a circle of rocks. The log ignited slowly but once afire, filled the end of the cave with light. The girls settled with their backs against the wall and watched the flickering light dance on the dark walls.

"Your Dad," Joanie said. "How can he protect them?"

"He's a ranger. Like a policeman, but out on the range. He helps animals as much as he helps people. He puts poachers in jail."

"Oh," Joanie said and then added, "but how can he fix this?"

"You don't know my Dad."

Joanie let out a long sigh. "There's no way I can sleep." Ten minutes later she nodded off, still sitting up.

Dana leaned her head back against the wall and listened to the soothing sound of the gurgling water. She closed her eyes and saw the unicorns in her mind, playing in a stream, bouncing and rearing up and racing across a wide plain.

But when sleep came to Dana, she didn't dream at all.

• • •

Dana's Dad was named Paul and he was in his khaki uniform as he stood at the back fence of the summer camp, a powerful flashlight in his left hand. He looked back at the girl standing next to Mrs. Miniver.

"What did Joanie tell you?" he asked.

The girl spoke quickly, explaining how Joanie bragged about a secret she and Dana has discovered out on the plain. "I think it was some kind of animal," the girl said.

Pointing the flashlight over the fence, Paul spotted footprints in the charcoal dust. Two sets of prints leading away from the wall, across the plateau.

He climbed the fence and went down on his haunches. There were other prints too. Hooves. He let out a relieved breath. No other human prints meant they'd gone off on their own and had not be taken away. And hooves were not the foot markings of a predator.

Turning back to the yard where his fellow rangers were assembled, he said, "OK. They walked off this way. Come on."

"They crossed the plain at night?" a worried ranger said as the men and women came forward with their flashlights.

"Come on." Paul led the way, slowly, carefully following the footprints. "You guys scatter in both directions as we go around the boulders. We can't lose these prints." He didn't have to say they couldn't wait until morning. Not with two little girls lost on the Charcoal Plain.

He forced himself to remain calm. He would find them, would never stop until he did. He whispered a silent prayer that the girls hadn't stumbled upon something bad. He reminded himself there were no known large predators on the eastern side of the northern hemisphere of Octavion. Not like the Sepia and Magenta Forests surrounding the pale blue Cerulean Sea of the southern hemisphere. He also reminded himself how Dana, always the adventurous one, was smart enough to be careful.

If kittens had hooves, he'd know why she crossed the dark plain at night.

Locating the tracks after reaching a patch of aqua grass was difficult. Suddenly there were other tracks, large tracks, lizard-like tracks, not hooves, not the girls' boots. Paul felt his heartbeat rising as he swung his flashlight around, then pointed it back at the large tracks. He couldn't identify the tracks. He was a police ranger, not a scientist, but whatever made the tracks was big. Could it be a predator?

"Oh, no," he said aloud, picking up his pace.

Then the plain became more rocky and there were no more tracks. The searchers stopped and gathered around Dana's Dad who called immediately for reinforcements on his radio.

"We need to spread out in twos. Keep in touch by radio and keep moving south by west," he told everyone. As they split up into pairs, he thought to himself that as soon as it was light, they'd get a hovercraft up in the sky.

Paul continued forward in the last direction the tracks seemed to lead. Shaking his head, he suddenly remembered the baby yellow finches in their backyard and how upset Dana became when a red killer-shrike, a particularly pretty bird, came into the yard and began to eat the baby finches. She threw rocks, dug out her brother's slingshot and stayed outside to guard the nest until a large Octavion Albatross came along and ran off the shrike, permanently.

• • •

A warmth on her face woke Dana, but it wasn't the fire log, which had gone out, but sunlight steaming into the cave. She stood and stepped toward the edge where the opening should have been only it glimmered so brightly, too brightly to look at. Dana had to shield her eyes from the golden glow, a shimmering, that bounced and danced. It was something magical, this shimmering light. Dana hesitated and reached out and her hand moved through the light and felt warm air beyond. She took in a deep breath and pushed her face through the light and looked out at an incredible sight. It took a moment for the dazzling colors to register.

The fall-off from the cave wasn't steep at all, with a trail descending to a silver river. There were shallows below with emerald boulders, the river so shallow you could see the bottom. Beyond lay fields of lime green grass separated by stands of dark blue Indigo trees with pale blue leaves and long rows of coral-leafed burgundy bushes. As she looked around Dana saw it was a deep valley surrounded by the Cranberry Hills. And grazing on the lime grass was a herd of unicorns. Two colts raced through the heard, rearing and shaking their heads, golden manes floating in the warm, early morning air.

Joanie stirred behind Dana but she didn't look back at her friend, captivated by the scene before her. Dana sat at the edge of the cave and watched. Joanie joined her and both sat without saying anything for a long time.

A half hour passed before Dana said, "We can't let anyone else see this."

"Huh?"

"If they do, they'll put them in zoos or kill them for their horns."

"No." Joanie's *no* sounded unsure.

Three unicorns moved to the river and drank, then began playing in the water, bouncing and splashing with a stomping of hooves. The three were joined by the colts and the play continued until all settled down and began to nibble the grass again, some eating the coral leaves of the burgundy bushes.

"I'm hungry," Joanie said, digging into the knapsack, pulling out the protein bars and two bottles of water.

"Bet that water down there is cooler," Dana said, then froze as she heard a noise behind them. The girls turned and looked into the cave as the sound came closer.

Footsteps and voices. Joanie moved closer to Dana as a man and a woman with blonde hair rounded the last turn of the cave and stopped. Both wore the same khaki uniform Dana's father wore. The woman took another step forward and squinted, having trouble seeing through the shimmering light. When she continued forward, Dana stepped toward her and the woman smiled immediately.

"You wouldn't happen to be Dana?"

Joanie let out a mousy sound and Dana nodded, feeling Joanie just behind her.

The woman pulled a radio from her belt and spoke into it. Dana heard her father's name as the woman stepped closer, " ... we have your daughter. Both girls are fine. We're in the southeast cave."

Putting the radio away, the woman asked, "You *are* all right?"

Dana's chin sank and left it to Joanie to say, "Yes. Are we in bad trouble?"

The woman smiled and asked if they were hungry or thirsty. The man hurried back through the cave as the woman stepped over and looked down at the valley.

"Lovely, isn't it?"

It took Dana's Dad ten minutes to arrive, jogging into the cave, stopping a few feet away to put his hand on his knees to catch his breath. His head bent forward, he took his time catching his breath. A bunch of men and some women, all in the same khaki uniforms stopped behind him.

When he stood, he opened his arms and Dana moved to them and he hugged her harder than he'd ever hugged her before. Then he went down on his knees and brushed her hair from her face and asked if she was really all right.

"Yes. It was my idea. We stayed here all night. Joanie wanted to go back, but I wouldn't let her."

"What ever possessed you to cross the plain like that?" His eyes became narrow. "Someone didn't bring you here did they?"

Dana shook her head, grabbed her Dad's hand and pulled him over to the cave's edge. She pointed down at the unicorns and said, "We followed them from the school."

Her Dad called back to the other rangers and several came forward with tools in their hands.

"What are you going to do?" Dana asked.

"We're going to seal off this cave and the other two to keep the unicorns from getting out on the plain again. That's what we've been doing these last few weeks, setting it up."

"Setting what up?"

Her father looked back at two men carrying a large piece of clear plastic.

"Come on, let's get out of the way." Her father led Dana and Joanie back through the cave. Dana suddenly stopped and said, "I'd like to say good-bye."

Her father smiled. "What for? Soon as they set up the viewing station we can come back and watch them any day."

"Viewing station?"

Her father prodded them along. "It's a miracle we've kept this a secret. Only way we can protect them is to keep them in their valley and let people watch them from the caves. Nobody goes in and nothing comes out."

"So you won't take them to a zoo?" Joanie finally found her voice.

"No. And no one will hurt them."

They stepped from the cave, passing more men carrying plastic sheets. Dana took her Dad's hand as they moved toward his land rover. "They are the most beautiful things I've ever seen Dad."

"Yes, but that big lizard whose tracks followed you two from the school wasn't very pretty."

"What big lizard?"

Her Dad stopped and pointed to the lizard tracks next to his land rover. The girls looked at it and he could see in their faces they wouldn't be crossing any plateaus at night again.

Before climbing into the land rover, Dana looked back at the cave. She closed her eyes and saw the unicorns again, their white horns glowing in the morning sunlight, silver horns shimmering and golden manes dancing as they raced across the bright green grass. She smiled, knowing she'd be back again and again, to watch them frolic in their secret valley.

THE END *of* **"Happy Living Things"**

for my daughter Dana

Upon a Painted Ocean

Day after day, day after day,
We stuck, nor breath nor motion;
As idle as a painted ship
Upon a painted ocean.

"The Rime of the Ancient Mariner"
Samuel Taylor Coleridge (Earth, 1798 a.d.)

"She's not a mermaid," Troy said. "She just lives in the ocean." He stood and dusted off his pants.

Sam watched his brother look down the low cliff to the beach below. Sam put his left hand over his eyes and looked down at the beach too. The white sand shimmered beneath the strong Octavion sun.

"She'll come out soon," Troy said.

Sam turned his gaze to the wide expanse of the Painted Ocean, at the deep blue water away from shore, at the subtle greens closer to shore, at the bright turquoise water along the beach. Beneath the water, he saw streaks of dark purple and crimson red and various shades of yellow – coral reefs.

He turned to his brother and saw how peaceful Troy looked.

"She's quite a woman," Troy said, his chest rising.

Sam shook his head and wondered what would cause Troy to believe anything lived in an Octavion ocean, except for fish, crustaceans, ichthyosaurs and elasmosaurs beyond the reefs.

A breeze, thick with the smell of salt water, washed over the brothers. The breeze blew through Troy's sandy hair as he stood at the cliff top, his fists on his sides now.

He looks thinner, Sam thought.

At six-four, Troy always looked slim. In his yearbook at St. Vincent's, Troy was described as *gangly*. Thirty-two now, he looked thinner than he did in high school.

Sam stood up and dusted off his pants. He stretched and tried not to think about how tired he was. Not quite six feet, Sam was thickly built with their mother's dark hair and eyes.

"Come on," Troy said and led the way down the cliff to the beach.

As soon as they reached the sand, Troy pulled off his canvas shoes and started for the rocks at the water's edge. Sam sat on a boulder and took off his boots and socks, which he stuffed into his boots. He fanned his khaki shirt, already dripping with sweat. The sand felt good between his toes, cooler than he thought it would. Sam walked behind his brother who stopped and let out a slight gasp and pointed to the water. Sam shielded his eyes again and saw a movement, saw something protrude from the water, between the waves. He started forward.

"It's her." Troy waved to his younger brother.

A head rose from the water, long light brown hair and a face as blue as the sky. She shook her head and her hair swished from side to side. She ran her hands, blue hands, through her hair as she continued forward.

Another step and the water fell away from her breasts. Another step and her flat belly came into view. She moved slowly and gracefully, following a small wave to shore and stood before the brothers. Naked, she had a perfectly shaped body – full breasts and round hips and long slender legs. Sam felt suddenly very awake. He felt his heart beating.

She smiled at Troy and then looked at Sam and craned her neck forward, as if to study him. Her eyes were the brightest green he'd ever seen – emerald eyes.

"The blue goes away," Troy said.

"Huh?"

"She changes colors." Troy reached his right hand for her. She took his hand, stepped into his arms and kissed him on the mouth.

Sam looked around, at the surf, at the sand, at the boulders and then up at the cliff before looking back at his brother kissing the naked blue woman. He rubbed his eyes, but she was still there when his vision returned. Their mouths opened against each other, their heads moving from side to side, their bodies pressed tightly together. Troy's hands slid down her back and caressed her ass.

Sam took in a deep breath and decided to wait back by his boots.

"Hey, where're you going?"

Sam pointed to his boots.

"Come on," Troy said as he led the blue woman by the hand, up the beach. "We'll sit on the rocks." He waved toward a group of flat boulders to Sam's left.

The woman sat back on the center boulder, her legs straight out, her hands behind her back, her breasts pointing up at the sun.

Troy sat close to her, his back to his brother.

Sam sat on the low boulder a little below them and watched the ocean. He sucked in a deep breath of humid, salty air.

"I told you she was quite a woman."

Sam nodded and shrugged and nodded again.

"Go on, look at her. See. She's changing color already."

Facing the sun, the woman's long hair streamed behind her in the slight breeze, the nipples of her full breasts were pointed. Troy was right, her skin was no longer blue, but seemed red.

"She'll turn pink and then flesh color." Troy touched her hair and she opened her eyes and smiled at him. "And her hair'll lighten until she's a blonde. Even her pubic hair."

Sam looked away from her pubic hair and noticed her toes were webbed. The movement of her hand drew Sam's gaze back up. She stroked Troy's face as her skin dried in the hot sun, as she turned pink and then slipped into a flesh color.

Sam watched the waves roll to shore. Looking up at the sky, he tried to spot a pesky pterodactyl, then reminded himself that it was true after all – there were no dinosaurs along the eastern hemisphere of Octavion – except in the oceans.

When he looked back at the woman, she was flesh-colored, her hair blonde, her pubic hair a shade darker. He felt his heartbeat rising. The woman leaned forward and kissed Troy, her hands unbuttoning his shirt. She pushed it off and reached for his pants. Troy pulled his mouth away and shrugged at his brother.

"We do this a lot," Troy managed to say as the woman began to shove his pants down.

Sam stood, put his hands into the back pockets of his pants and walked back up the beach. At the base of the cliff, he stopped and tied his boots together and draped them over his shoulder. He climbed the cliff, the rocks somewhat cooler on his feet. At the top, he took a look down and they were at it all right, there on the flat boulder, the surf rolling to shore next to them.

He went to his brother's cabin and opened a cold beer.

• • •

Sam just finished his second beer when the door banged open and Troy stumbled in. Naked and pale, Troy fell to his knees and looked at his brother with a crooked smile, then slowly sank forward on the floor.

Sam pulled Troy up on the sofa and his brother coughed and grabbed the front of his shirt.

"She's quite . . . a . . . woman." Troy let go of the shirt, coughed again and managed to say, "I'll be all right. After some sleep." And he curled up in a fetal position on the sofa, the crooked smile back on his lips.

Sam went to the door but didn't see the woman. He walked across the lawn to the cliff; and she was down there on the rock, lying spread-eagle. He went back to his hovercraft and pulled out his binoculars. Focusing them on the woman he saw her move slightly.

She wasn't flesh colored anymore, she was as pale as Troy. Or maybe that was the sunlight?

Sam watched her chest rise and fall as she breathed and felt a chill along his back.

What is she?

On his way back to the cabin, Sam reached into the hovercraft and took out his nine-millimeter Glock.

He checked his brother's pulse, and it was fine. He checked his brother's forehead and felt no fever. So he sat in the easy chair, facing the door, the gun in his lap.

Bone weary from the trip, all Sam wanted was sleep as well. But he felt goose bumps on his arms when he thought about the woman. He figured he should call the Institute about her right away, or the Coast Guard. Or maybe he should call the university in Scarlet City.

His eyes burned from lack of sleep. He closed them for a moment. When he felt himself drifting, he got up and checked on Troy who had rolled over on his belly.

Yawning and stretching, Sam spotted a movement in the door and wheeled. She stood in the doorway, leaning her right hand on the door frame, her shoulder drooped forward. Pallid white, she seemed wobbly as she stood blinking at him.

He looked at the Glock on the easy chair. When he looked back at her, she was looking at Troy. Sam took two quick steps, scooped up his gun and pointed it at her.

She twisted her head toward him and blinked again. He raised the Glock; but she didn't seem to notice it. He slipped his finger through the trigger guard and ticked the trigger.

"Just stay where you are," he said.

She blinked again and smiled weakly.

He looked into her eyes. She wasn't human but he saw nothing alien whatsoever in those green eyes. Her wide eyes looked childlike, her stare unwavering. She moved toward him slowly, brushing her hair back with her hands, her hips rolling as she stepped toward him.

Sam backed away, all the way to the wall. He pointed the Glock between her breasts and gritted his teeth.

"Don't come any closer," he heard himself say as he began to squeeze the trigger. She continued forward and he knew he wouldn't shoot. He lowered the gun as she stopped in front of him. She pulled her long hair away from her face and turned her head slightly, parting her lips, closing her eyes.

Sam heard the Glock hit the floor. He licked his lips and looked at hers only an inch away. She was beautiful . . . damn beautiful.

"Hey!" His brother's voice brought him back.

Troy was sitting up now and rubbing his belly. "How about getting some steaks out of the refrigerator? I'm starving."

The woman inched away from Sam. Turning to Troy, she smiled and moved to him and curled up on the sofa next to him, her head on his shoulder.

Troy grinned at Sam and said, "She's mute. Did I tell you?"

"No." Sam wiped his sweaty hands on his shirt.

"Actually she makes a whistling sound when we make love, but she doesn't talk like us."

Sam nodded and moved on shaky legs into the kitchen. He found fresh steaks and two large potatoes and more beer.

"Does she eat steaks?"

"I don't know what she eats. She eats in the sea."

• • •

She sat next to Troy, across the table from Sam and watched them eat. Her eyes darting, she rested her chin in the palm of her hand, her elbow on the table. The woman crossed her arms beneath her breasts. Sam couldn't help thinking there was something fine and regal in her pose, the way she sat and turned her head, looking back and forth at the brothers.

"I call her Wanda," Troy said. "Remember Wanda?"

Sam shrugged and put his fork down. "She answer to that name? I mean, she understand when you call her?"

Troy shook his head and shoved another chuck of steak into his mouth.

Sam picked up his fork and took another bite, savoring the sharp taste of cooked meat. Crisp on the outside and juicy inside, it was very good. Only he couldn't keep his hands from shaking. Not enough to be noticed, but Sam felt jittery inside.

He reached for his beer and said, "The Institute's worried about you."

Troy shrugged.

"Your last samples and reports were sub-par."

Troy looked at Wanda and winked.

Sam felt his nerves start up again. He looked at Wanda and she gave him that regal look and he heard himself telling his brother,

"You realize that . . . uh . . . she's the most amazing . . . creature . .
. ever found on Octavion."

"Obviously." Troy grinned and blinked his light eyes. "She's
quite a woman."

After dinner, as Sam slipped his dish into the dishwasher, he
heard Troy and Wanda get up from the table and move into the
living room. He added his brother's plate to the dishwasher and
cleaned up the table.

He stepped into the living room just as Troy rolled on top of
Wanda on the sofa.

"Uh," Sam said, and then went out. His hands still shaking, he
stopped and leaned on the porch rail for a moment. In the distance
the sun was sinking. Sam sucked in a deep breath and went to the
cliff to watch the huge Octavion sun slip into the Painted Ocean.

The beauty of this treacherous world never ceased to amaze
him. From its primeval forests and crystal seas, to its brightly
colored hills and wondrous waterfalls, Octavion was the greatest
mystery of the galaxy. A world inhabited by dinosaurs. A world to
puzzle the greatest scientists.

Why?

Was this Earth as it was millions of years ago? Is this why it is
here?

Someone once said the reason humans have flocked to
Octavion was a search for Earth's past beauty. Sam had no idea.
He and his brother were born here.

The shimmering orange orb seemed to sizzle as it fell along
the distant horizon, turning the ocean violet and green and then
purple. The waters gradually slipped into a deep navy blue before
fading into gray and then into a blackness as black as sack-cloth.

The moonless Octavion night came as thick as a veil. Sam
leaned back on his elbow and watched the stars come out – first
one, then another, then so many it looked truly like a Milky Way.

He lay back, his hands under his head and closed his eyes. He
felt his steady breathing rid him of the jitters, lull him until he
remembered Wanda – the real Wanda. Sam opened his eyes to the
dark sky and let his mind roll back to dusty Bone Street back when

they were boys. Wanda lived across the street. She was Troy's first sweetheart.

The more he thought about it, the more the blue woman looked like Wanda all grown up. Sitting up, he looked back at the cabin. Rising slowly, his knees stiff from exhaustion, Sam walked back to the cabin and looked in through the open front door. They were asleep on the sofa, their arms and legs entangled.

He went in and picked up the Glock. Standing over them, he had to look closely to see they were both breathing. Even more pale than before, they looked wasted. Sam felt the hair standing along the back of his neck. He started to raise the Glock again, but fell back and moved out of the cabin again. He walked over to the cliff and sat heavily and looked out at the dark waters, the Glock cradled in his lap. The bright stars shimmered on the black-as-oil surface of the Painted Ocean. The water moved like living tar.

He smelled the salt in the damp air. Closing his tired eyes, he tried to think, tried to clear his weary mind.

What am I going to do?

He felt he had to do something, something drastic. That was his brother. He closed his eyes and thought back, again, to the dusty days of their youth, of sleeping in the same bed as kids, taking turns fanning the sheets to keep cool during the hot Octavion nights.

He remembered running. They ran everywhere, kicking up dust in their wake. He could see himself and Troy running, their skinny bodies lithe and young and full of mischief.

Sam closed his eyes, his throat tight with emotion.

Something was happening to his big brother. He had to do something.

Sam started to rise and saw another vision in his mind. He saw a pair of wide brown eyes so dark they looked black, and the round face of Thea as she smiled shyly at him, her small, soft mouth pouty and so beautiful.

He still missed her. He always missed her. For the millionth time, he remembered the face of his first love – a love that had drifted away, as fragile as a snowflake on a planet that never knew snow. For the millionth time he tried to figure how it fell apart, how it just blew away, like the dust from the street where he used run as a boy.

• • •

Sam heard Troy's voice and stirred and woke suddenly in the bright light of the Octavion dawn. Rising as he lay next to the cliff, he felt dizzy for a moment in confusion, then saw Troy waving at him from the cabin.

"Come on," Troy called out. "I need help!"

Sam stumbled up, reached down and picked up the Glock, his back cracking. He hurried over to the cabin as Troy went back inside. By the time he reached the front door, Troy had Wanda up and was trying to walk her out.

"We got to get her to the ocean." Troy blinked his sunken eyes at Sam and struggled forward. He looked even more pale now. Wanda hung lifelessly against him, her skin as white as chalk.

"Help me!" Troy gasped as he and Wanda fell forward.

Sam dropped the Glock and caught them and took most of Wanda's weight in his arm. Grabbing her around the waist, he lifted her and led the way down the three porch steps and across the grass to the cliff.

Troy faltered only once on the way down, but grunted and he kept up.

Sam took all of Wanda's weight in his arm as they moved slowly down to the beach.

"Hurry," Troy gasped.

They stumbled across the sand to the water, the early morning sun already casting their long shadows. As soon as the warm water struck their legs, Wanda moaned.

"All the way in," Troy said, falling away for a moment. He pulled Wanda and Sam into the surf until they were waist deep.

"Dunk her." Troy shoved at Wanda and Sam helped shove her under the water. She sank and rose immediately with the next wave.

"Move her!" Troy pushed her; and Sam grabbed her shoulders and pulled her. A larger wave slammed into Sam's back and shoved Wanda away momentarily. He pulled her back and felt her move with him now.

The next two waves, gentler, seemed to bring more movement to Wanda until she twisted and turned away from them and slipped away slowly.

"She's going be all right," Troy said, wiping water from his face. He looked at Sam with glassy eyes and wavered as he stood. Sam grabbed him just as Troy swooned, and carried his big brother all the way back up the cliff to the cabin.

Catching his breath after dropping Troy on his bed, Sam moved back down the hall to the sofa to collapse himself, his arms aching and his legs twitching from overexertion.

Sam felt himself drifting into a deep sleep.

When he woke, with a start, he moved stiffly back to the bedroom. Troy was still asleep. Leaving the bathroom door open, Sam took a long, hot shower, brushing his teeth, climbing into a fresh shirt and pants. The shirt's crisp starch felt clean on his bare back, the cotton pants soft against his legs.

He put a pot of coffee on and watched it brew, pulling a steamy cup away as soon as it was ready. Strong and black, the coffee bit his tongue and warmed him immediately. Sam went out on the front porch and sat on the steps and drank his coffee as he watched the multicolored ocean move to shore and then out again.

He heard a movement behind him, turned and saw Troy with a mug of coffee cradled in both hands.

"You quit wearing clothes altogether?" Sam leaned against the porch railing.

Troy nodded, took a shaky sip and cleared his throat. "I . . . uh . . . got something to tell you." He took another sip of coffee, then said, "I'm going to live with Wanda." He focused his light eyes on Sam. "In the ocean."

Sam stood, his throat suddenly dry.

"I don't mean right now," Troy said with a weak smile. "I'm too hungry." He turned and over his shoulder said he was going to make pancakes and hot sausage.

Sam followed him in, sitting at the kitchen table after he poured himself another cup of coffee.

"Remember the first time we tried making pancakes?" Troy shot Sam a mischievous grin.

Sam nodded. They nearly set fire to their mother's kitchen. He was eight.

"I'm a better cook now," Troy said, working two pans, one with pancakes, one sizzling with sausage. The sweet smell of cooked meat filled the room immediately. Sam felt his stomach rumble.

"Ow," Troy backed away from the stove. "Hand me the screen in there."

Sam dug out the mesh grease screen and passed it to Troy who put it over the frying pan.

"Ow!" Troy stepped back again. "Go get me a shirt."

As Sam stepped into the hall, he turned and walked backwards, watching the front door. He quickly pulled a red shirt off a hanger and grabbed a pair of Troy's pants that were draped over a chair in the bedroom and hurried back down the hall.

The sausage sizzled, the pancakes bubbled and the kitchen door was wide open.

Sam dropped the clothes and ran out. He bolted around to the front of the cabin and across to the cliff. Troy was nearly at the beach. Sam hurried down the path. Slipping, he slammed his right knee on a boulder and took a moment to recover. Limping, he half-fell, half-ran down the cliff. He hit the beach running, but Troy was already knee-deep in the surf.

Wanda, all blue again, stood waist deep in water, her arms outstretched for Troy. He lunged for her and she wrapped her arms around him.

"Troy! Troy! Troy!" Sam's feet dug into the sand.

Troy, still hugging Wanda, turned their bodies and looked at his brother and smiled and sank into the water.

"No!" Sam fell into the surf, rose and stumbled forward and dove for the spot they had disappeared. The warm, salt water stung his face momentarily and he blinked and his vision cleared.

Sinking deeper, he spotted movement to his left and pulled himself toward it.

He saw feet – Troy's feet and Wanda's blue legs.

They moved away quickly, too quickly.

Sam kicked his legs and pulled with his arms and surged after them.

He lost sight of them in the turbulence trailing behind their legs. He pushed himself and felt his hand strike something. He rolled to the side and saw it was Troy's foot. He grabbed it and held on.

The foot pulled him. Sam held on with both hands. The foot dragged him and then stopped and then, incredibly, slipped out of his fingers. He struggled to catch it again, but his lungs ached and he felt lightheaded.

He looked around and saw them, a distance away now and much lower, near a yellow reef. Hand in hand, Troy and Wanda stood on the ocean floor looking at him.

Sam dove for them. He pulled at the water and pushed his weakening legs. His air slipped out as he dove, bubbles leaking out of his mouth and his lungs felt as if they would explode.

He hurt. The pain was so intense and he fought it, fought against the water and then . . . he slammed into a wall of blackness and felt himself floating.

He felt hands on his arms and hands touching his legs as he drifted.

He tried to breath.

Sharp salt water slammed into his mouth and he gagged.

• • •

The heat on his face caused Sam to blink.

Sunlight in his eyes and sand against his face – he tried to raise his head. It took a couple tries before he slowly crawled up on his knees. He felt the wet inside his clothes, against his skin, although they were dry outside. He rolled over on his back and brushed the sand from his right cheek.

Sam looked out at the turquoise waves and the shades of deep green water beyond. His throat burned. It took so much strength to stand, he had to widen his stance to keep his wobbly knees from folding. He waited long seconds until he could move.

Sam walked to the edge of the water and cupped his hands over his eyes and looked at the Painted Ocean, at the waves, at the water, at the void where his brother disappeared.

His brother.

He felt a pain in his chest, felt his eyes burning with tears, felt so empty inside and so helpless. He fell back on his rump and sank back on the sand and covered his eyes with his arms.

Bone Street – running behind his big brother in the dust, never able to catch Troy as they ran and played through endless days. Bone Street – following Troy around meeting other kids, stealing a first kiss beneath a yellow streetlight until their mother called them in. Bone Street – laughing so hard his side ached. Troy always, *always* made him laugh.

The hovercraft.

Sam sat up. He stood and stumbled up the beach. Catching himself, he went up the cliff on all fours. His arms were weak, his legs throbbing, he struggled to catch his breath. He tumbled to the top and crawled a few feet on the cool grass before standing. He jogged over to the hovercraft.

Maybe, he thought, he could spot them. Maybe he could spot Troy in the crystalline water. He smelled smoke and looked over at the cabin. A cloud of smoke filtered out the kitchen door; and he remembered the sausages and pancakes. He shook his dizzy head.

Let it burn, he told himself.

Climbing in the hovercraft, he moved to the controls and fell heavily in the pilot's seat. Sam's shaky fingers bounced across the computer panel. Lights came on inside the craft and the engine hummed to life and a hand fell on Sam's left shoulder.

He jumped and turned around to a pair of brown eyes so dark they looked like black star-sapphires. The woman pulled back and blinked at him, twisted her head slightly, her pouty lips pursed. Her hair was longer and her face rounder, her skin pale blue, but it was Thea – all grown up. She took two steps backward. Sam climbed out of the pilot's seat. The woman stared at him as she inched away, the sunlight bathing her pale-blue skin with dazzling white light.

A movement in the doorway caused Sam to turn. Troy's face leaned in, smiling as he said, "How do you like her?"

Sam moved around the co-pilot's chair and fell toward the door. Troy moved back out of his way and Sam jumped out. Troy stood, arms folded, his skin a deep, suntanned color now.

"You're all right?" Sam reached forward and grabbed his brother's shoulders to make sure he was there.

"I told you it would be all right." Troy punched Sam's shoulder lightly. "Hey, you almost let my cabin burn down." He pointed over his shoulder to Wanda coming out of the cabin. She was still pale blue.

Sam grabbed his brother's arm and said. "You're all right?"

"Humans don't change colors," Troy said. It took a second for Sam to figure what he meant.

"But . . ."

"Hey, I don't understand it either. But I could breath underwater. It was like my skin was absorbing oxygen straight from the water. I could feel it."

Wanda came up and tucked her arms around Troy's. She closed her eyes and faced the sun, her skin reddening as she stood.

Sam heard a movement behind him and turned back as the blue Thea climbed out of the hovercraft.

Leaning her back against it, she too faced the sun and her skin reddened. She shook out her dark hair, which showed brown highlights in the sunshine. Her hands pressed against the doorway, her feet parted slightly, her lips were extra pouty and so dark red they looked like over-ripe cherries. And her skin became flesh-colored and she *was* Thea, all grown up.

"She's a beauty, isn't she?" Troy said, reaching over to tousle his brother's hair, as he'd done a million times before.

Sam looked down at her soft neck, at her full breasts and down to her round hips and thick mat of dark pubic hair, and down her shapely legs.

She was beautiful.

When he looked back up, the dark eyes were staring at him. Unblinking, round and luminous, the dark orbs stared at him with such a sadness. It surprised Sam. A tear fell from her left eye and rolled down her cheek. She blinked and a tear fell from her right eye.

She bit her lower lip and pushed herself away from the hovercraft. Reaching her right hand out hesitatingly, she stepped toward Sam. He took in a deep breath just as the tips of her fingers touched the side of his neck, pulled back and then touched his left cheek gently, very gently.

He heard Troy whispering to Wanda and felt them move away.

Thea's fingers rubbed the stubble of his beard.

Staring deeply into her eyes, Sam felt his heart thundering in his ears. He felt the dark jewels of her eyes pull him, caress him. He felt the heat of the sun on his head. He felt a coolness coming from her and a sweet smell of perfume, an hypnotic scent as sweet as any perfume he'd ever smelled on any woman.

Another tear rolled out of her right eye and she pulled her hand away from his face and wiped the tear off her cheek. She inched closer, right against him, and raised her arms around his neck. She pulled him to her and hugged him.

Gently, she hugged him, her body barely touching his, for long seconds. Then, slowly, she pulled her head back and looked into his eyes again. He felt her breath on his lips. She tilted her head slightly; and her lips parted like the petals of a flower and she kissed him. So softly, she kissed his lips as softly as velvet.

He kissed her back and felt her tongue touch his. He worked his tongue back against hers. He felt her body press against him, her hands moved up and down his neck. He put his hands on her hips and her skin was as silky as satin.

Sam felt a well of emotion in his chest, a tightness in his throat as they kissed. He felt tears roll out of his eyes and tried to catch his breath without ending the kiss.

It was too pleasurable. *Too* pleasurable.

Sam felt a shudder along his back. He pushed his hands against her hips and tried to pull away, but could not.

She pulled him tighter, rubbing her body against him. He felt the weight of her breasts pressing him, the point of her pubic bone against his left thigh. He felt his hands cup her ass and squeeze as she kissed him deeper.

Fight it – he told himself. He remembered Troy's pale skin after loving Wanda.

Fight it.

He pulled his mouth away and gasped for breath. She pulled him back, kissing his lips furiously, again and again.

Fight it. And yet, he kissed her back, just as furiously.

Finally, Thea pulled away and smiled at him. Gasping for breath, Sam tried to look away from her eyes, but could not. He found himself staring deeply into the darkness of her mesmerizing eyes as she pulled back and unbuttoned his shirt. She shoved his shirt off and pressed her breasts back against him and they were so hot and firm.

Fight it.

He felt her heart pounding against his chest as she closed her eyes and they kissed again. And it felt so damn wonderful.

Fight it – he told himself. *Fight it.*

He *would* fight it. He *would* fight it.

THE END *of* **"Upon a Painted Ocean"**

Things Both Great and Small

He prayeth best, who loveth best
All things both great and small;
For the dear God who loveth us,
He made and loveth all.

"The Rime of the Ancient Mariner"
Samuel Taylor Coleridge (Earth, 1798 a.d.)

Vincent and Dana lived with their father in a stone house on a dusty street at the edge of Bronze Town, next to the rocky, Terra Cotta Plateau on planet Octavion's north-eastern hemisphere. Their house, like most of the town, was built of the bronze-colored stone gathered from the vast plateau. Their backyard fence was also made of bronze stone, lined inside with bushes of burnished-gold with small, teal leaves and two trees their father transplanted from the Indigo Forest five years ago. The trees had dark blue bark and pale blue leaves.

After school, Dana could be found playing in their grassless backyard while Vincent took off for Russet Butte and the caverns. He'd discovered the caverns a year ago but only recently found the cavern with the rear opening that overlooked the Majestic Blue River and the rolling grasslands of the vast, Sage Plain and the dark green trees of the Spearmint Forest.

Lying on his belly at the cavern's mouth, fourteen-year-old Vincent would gaze down the one-hundred-foot cliff to the river below, watching its deep blue water rushing past. He could scan the Sage Plain for one of the plant eaters, a Stegosaur or a Nodosaur. Once, he'd caught a glimpse of a predator, a juvenile tyrannosaur about six feet tall, perfectly camouflaged for the Spearmint Forest with its green stripes. It stepped out on the plain and sniffed the air, then ducked back into the forest. It was the most magnificent creature Vincent had ever seen. He talked about it for weeks and returned every day, hoping for another glimpse.

124

One afternoon, as he approached the butte on his bicycle, Vincent saw tires tracks in the dust. He slowed and followed the tracks around the great rocks outside the cavern's entrance and almost ran into a land rover, hidden between the rocks. The rover had a fender missing.

He looked inside and saw it was empty. He felt the hood and it wasn't hot at all. Vincent hid his bike and crept into the cavern, listening carefully for any noise. Taking the familiar turns, he smelled the fresh air coming through the far end of the cavern, smelled the rich, sweet scent of the Spearmint Forest.

Peeking around the final turn, he spotted a large pulley and a rope near the opening. Inching closer, he saw the rope was tied to the largest boulder inside the cavern. Vincent inched closer and spotted the rope ladder. He went down on his belly and crawled to the opening and looked down. The ladder went all the way to the ground. A movement below caught his eyes and he pulled back. Several thundering heartbeats later, he peeked over the edge again and saw a woman with long blond hair sitting next to the river, her feet in the water.

Like Vincent, she wore a khaki shirt and shorts. Leaning back on her hands, her long hair falling over her shoulders, she lifted her chin skyward. Vincent inched back until only his eyes and forehead peered over the edge.

The woman swung her feet back and forth in the water and rolled her shoulders slowly. A loud squawk from above made Vincent flinch as two pterodactyls swooped in from the Spearmint Forest. Not large enough to attack a human, the bat-like creatures still look fearsome. They fluttered away, downriver. As Vincent watched them, he spotted a large, orange inflatable boat heading up the river, toward the blonde lady, who was now standing and waving. Someone waved back and Vincent put his hands over his eyes to cut the sun's glare as he watched the odd-shaped boat approach. As it neared, Vincent saw the boat wasn't odd-shaped at all. A large black and red object, carried in the center of the boat caused it to lean to one side.

Shrill voices echoed below, excited voices. There were two men on the boat and as it came closer Vincent recognized the large black and red object. The hairs stood on the back of his neck.

It was a head, a bloody triceratops head.

Poachers.

Vincent crawled backward and stood. He tried to untie the rope ladder, but the rope was far too thick. The rope on the pulley was even thicker. If only he'd brought his folding knife. He turned and ran out of the cave for his bicycle. He could reach his father's office in a half hour easily. Jumping on his bike, he looked at the land rover.

Disable it. He jumped off his bike and ran to the front of the rover.

How to disable it?

Vincent looked back at the cave opening and knew what he had to do. He ran back in and pulled up the rope ladder as fast as he could. Ignoring the shouting from below, he ran back out to his bike and took off for town. Peddling hard across the rocky, Terra Cotta Plateau, he stopped by his house for his buck knife before continuing to his father's office.

The *Town Constable* sign above the entrance to the jail, another bronze stone building, this one near the center of town, leaned slightly off-kilter. Vincent ran past Mrs. Abigail, right into his father's office. Vincent's father looked up from the papers on his desk.

"Dad!" Vincent gasped, fighting to catch his breath.

"What's the problem?"

Vincent shook his head and pointed outside.

"Poachers!"

His father stared into Vincent's dark brown eyes. "Where?"

"Russet … Butte. Through the … cavern. They're down by … the river. They have the head of a triceratops."

His father's green eyes narrowed.

"How many?"

"Two men and a woman."

Vincent's father reached into his desk drawer and pulled out his stun pistol, slipping it into its holster on his right hip. He wore his familiar khaki shirt with its gold badge and dark blue pants. On their way out, his father took a stun rifle from the locker and told Mrs. Abigail where he was headed.

"Want me to call for backup?" she asked.

Vincent's father picked up a portable radio and told her if he needed backup, he'd call in.

Lifting Vincent's bike into the back of the white land cruiser, they climbed in and strapped their seatbelts. On the way Vincent explained about the land rover hidden behind the boulder and the extra-thick rope and pulley and the rope ladder.

"You pulled the rope ladder back up?" His father said with a nervous smirk.

"Yeah!"

"Good."

Dust billowed behind the cruiser as they crossed the rocky plateau, closing in quickly on the reddish-brown Russet Butte. Parking against the rear bumper of the land rover, blocking it in, they jumped out and walked into the cavern.

"Keep back." Vincent's father cautioned as he stepped to the opening and looked down.

"Police!" he called down. "I want you to come up one at a time. And stay away from those rifles!"

He tossed the rope ladder back down and stood with his stun rifle cradled in his arms. Vincent stepped to the far edge of the opening and glanced down. The two men stood next to the boat, which was tied to the bank now. The woman moved slowly to the rope and began climbing.

Vincent stared at the triceratops head, at the huge green horns and the great beak, much like that of a parrot.

"Why did they do that?" Vincent said.

"It's a trophy. Like the bad old days."

Vincent didn't understand, which must have shown on his face because his father explained, "Before they passed the Indigenous Creature Act, people hunted dinosaurs here all the time. Some for

127

food, but most for sport. Hang a T-Rex head on your living room wall."

"Rich people, huh?"

"Not just the rich."

Vincent nodded. He understood the dinosaurs of Octavion had to be protected. His science teacher explained how scientists were still trying to learn why there were creatures very much like Earth's dinosaurs here along the backwash of the Milky Way Galaxy.

"What are you going to do with the head?" Vincent asked.

As if in response, the two pterodactyls swooped down and landed on the head and ripped at its flesh.

"After the pterodactyls are finished with it, we'll get it over to First Colony City, to the university."

Reaching the top of the ladder, the woman blinked a pair of wide, blue eyes at Vincent's father, who helped her up and handcuffed her behind her back, asking her to stand against the wall. She turned her pretty face away from Vincent's peering stare. He was embarrassed too and looked away.

One of the men was already on the ladder, climbing slowly, when a sharp roar caused everyone to turn to the Spearmint Forest. Vincent spotted it first, a juvenile tyrannosaur stepped from the forest its green-striped body hunched forward.

It roared again and bolted for the river.

The man nearest the boat started running for the ladder. Another movement caught Vincent's eye as a second juvenile tyrannosaur surfaced in the river and leaped up the bank, not twenty yards behind the man running for the ladder.

The beast was awesome in it quick ferocity, glistening wet in the bright sunlight. It was … magnificent.

When the stun rifle fired next to Vincent, he jumped.

Vincent's father, standing at the edge of the cave opening, pointed his stun rifle again at the fast-moving tyrannosaur. He fired and a bolt of orange struck the tyrannosaur's chest. It didn't slow the beast. The man on the ground screamed.

"It won't stop!" His father said.

"Good," Vincent said.

Another orange bolt struck the tyrannosaur, with no effect.

Vincent turned to his father again and watched him twist the dial on the side of the rifle, go down on one knee and fire again. The tyrannosaur screeched, and tumbled forward. It tried to get up, but stumbled, its neck streaked with bright red blood. Vincent felt his heart stammering in his chest as he looked at the dying tyrannosaur twitching in agony.

The man reached the ladder just as the second tyrannosaur leaped from the river and raced at an incredible speed, closing fast on the man who climbed rapidly.

The tyrannosaur reached the ladder so fast the man was barely beyond its snapping jaws. Roaring loudly, the great beast tore at the rope ladder and both men held on. Vincent saw his father move to his right and level the rifle at the tyrannosaur. The rope ladder shook violently, the men screaming, the beast roaring as it ripped the ropes. The lower man dangled.

Another *pop* from the rifle and Vincent watched the tyrannosaur fall to the ground, its head nearly severed. Sitting back, Vincent felt as if he would throw up. He saw the woman sitting back against the wall, her eyes shut as she cried.

He could smell the blood now and wretched again, but managed to keep his food down. Vincent watched his father help the poachers up, handcuffing each, standing them against the side wall before going back to the cavern's entrance to look down at the tyrannosaurs.

Vincent crawled back to the edge and peered down at the sickening carnage. Both tyrannosaurs lay sprawled on the ground, neither moving. Vincent wiped sweat from his eyes and looked up at his father standing with clenched fists.

When he saw the look on his son's face, his shoulders sank.

"I had to," his father said in a voice barely above a whisper.

"Why? They're *poachers*."

"I can't let someone die."

"But they deserved to." Vincent's stomach felt sour as he looked at his father, who'd just killed *two tyrannosaurs*. After a

129

long moment, he turned away from his father's stare. Loud squawks focused Vincent attention back to the sky. A dozen pterodactyls bounced in the hot air above the carcasses. One landed on the horn of the triceratops and let out an even louder squawk.

"I can't let a human die," his father said. "Even bad ones."

Vincent looked at the three handcuffed poachers. None would return his stare. Standing slowly, he looked again at his father and saw pain in those familiar eyes and realized how much it must have hurt his father to pull that trigger.

THE END *of* **"Things Both Great and Small"**

for my son Vincent

Were Yellow as Gold

Her lips were red, *her* looks were free,
Her locks were yellow as gold:
Her skin was as white as leprosy,
The Night-mare LIFE-IN-DEATH was she

"The Rime of the Ancient Mariner"
Samuel Taylor Coleridge (Earth, 1798 a.d.)

It was the tide, lapping against his bare feet that opened Paul's eyes. He shut them immediately against the blinding sunlight reflecting off the white sand and struggled to sit up. His arms ached and his legs burned as if he'd just finished a marathon.

Shielding his eyes from the strong Octavion sun, Paul looked out at the bright sea, sky blue in the distance, dark blue with purplish splotches close to shore. And he remembered. This was the Cerulean Sea and the storm that attacked their yacht was long gone, attacking another part of the sparsely-populated Western Hemisphere of this damn planet of incredible beauty and sudden savagery.

Closing his eyes, Paul could almost feel the storm again, slamming against his face, peppering the sea with a million raindrops, tossing their boat about. He remembered the captain arrogantly calling it a *squall,* until the waves struck. Paul saw the final, giant wave, a vast mountain of white capped water rolling toward them, from the starboard side, felt the *Lydia* roll and break up, the salt water burning his throat. Paul broke the surface and gasped for air, the rain against his face, like hornet stings.

Opening his eyes again, Paul wiped the sand from his face and dusted off his crewman uniform, white shirt with blue stripes and blue shorts. His sneakers were gone, so was his watch. Suddenly, he remembered today was his eighteenth birthday. He was alive, by a miracle, he was alive. He ran his hands through his dark brown hair. Looking up and then down the long beach, he saw

131

something in the distance, something that appeared red. A life jacket? It took him nearly a minute to get to his feet. His legs quivered as he stood and painfully began walking to the red object on the beach.

The sand was so hot, he moved to the water's edge to walk in the surf and watched the waves break over a natural reef in the distance. The air was rich with the salty smell of the sea. A breeze flowed back from the land, filled with the scent of chlorophyll. Turning to the jungle on his left, he recognized the twisted branches of mangroves next to the beach and the purplish-red tree line beyond, an obvious extension of the vast Magenta Forest.

As the red object took form, he realized it was a body, but it wasn't wearing a life jacket. It was a red dress and her white legs pointed toward the sea, her long blonde hair matted around her head. She lay on her side, her back to him, a red high heel still on her right foot.

Paul stopped next to her and fell to his knees.

He cautiously touched her shoulder and she stirred. He gently brushed her hair from her face. The strands of her hair, glimmering in the sunlight, were yellow as gold between his fingers. He recognized her immediately. She was the beautiful blonde woman from the yacht, the one who never went out on deck during the day to keep her fair skin from burning. She'd slept her days below deck. He passed her once below deck on the long yacht. She never looked at him.

A wave sloshed up and took her shoe off. Paul grabbed it. Looking back, he realized he could see up her dress. Her white panties were damp and her ass plainly visible through the thin fabric.

Paul felt his heart racing as he moved around her.

She stirred again, letting out a long sigh.

My God, she was gorgeous.

Her eyes opened and blinked and she slowly sat up. She seemed to look through Paul as she sat back. He tried not to gasp when her left breast fell out of her torn dress. She wavered as she sat, then fell back to the sand on her back and lay there, the waves running up to her knees now.

As Paul leaned over her, his shadow falling across her face, he could see she was unconscious again. He stared at her exposed breast as it rose and fell with her breathing, at her small nipple and light pink areola. Suddenly, Paul felt a surge of energy as he slid his hands under her and picked her up and carried her to the shades of the mangroves. Lying her on her back, he collapsed next to her.

He didn't lose consciousness and eventually felt strong enough to sit up again. He carefully covered her breast with her dress but couldn't stop from staring at the front of her panties as she lay with her dress bunched up to her waist, a sliver of her darker-than-blonde public hair protruding from the sides of her panties.

A loud squawk turned Paul's gaze back to the sea. A half dozen pterodactyls circled the water above the reef. One plunged into the sea and surfaced immediately, beating its bat-like wings as it rose into the sky. Looking back at the mangroves, Paul wondered if this was an island or part of the mainland and more importantly, if there were predators lurking in the Magenta Forest.

Raptors were common to the forest and dimetrodons even more common to mangroves. Shielding his eyes again, Paul could see a hill beyond the mangroves. Maybe he could climb it and see if this was indeed an island. Wiping the sweat from his face, he swallowed hard, knowing he'd have to find water as soon as possible.

Making sure she was still in the shade, Paul picked up her shoe and eased his way into the mangroves.

• • •

Careful not to spill one precious drop of the spring water, Paul lifted her head and touched her shoe to her pink lips. The water sloshed against her lips and she opened them and sipped. Her pale blue eyes opened and she drank the rest of the water from the shoe, then sat up and blinked at Paul, who sat back on the sand. She looked around, wiped the sand from her face. As she readjusted her dress, the dress tore open and her breast was exposed again.

Before Paul could look away she caught him and snapped, "Pervert!"

If you were a man, Paul wanted to say, *or a sheep, I'd be a pervert,* but he couldn't say it aloud. He averted his eyes, looking down at the sand.

She straightened her dress and held the torn flap tight against her body.

"Where's the rest of the water?" she asked.

He pointed to the mangroves and explained there was a spring at the bottom of the hill and that they were on an island. He'd climbed the hill and was happy to see the island was too small for any large predators. He hoped.

She shook her head. "I mean where's the canteen you used?"

He lifted the empty shoe.

Her nose crinkled. "You gave me water from my shoe?" She looked at the beach again. "Where is everyone else?"

Paul shrugged and looked around the beach too.

"You mean ..." her voice trailed off.

She stood with difficulty, one hand keeping the dress closed, and took several shaky steps toward the water. Moving back into the shade, she put her free hand on her hip and glared at Paul.

"I can't walk around like this. Find me some clothes."

"Huh?"

"Something probably washed up by now." She pointed to the empty beach.

Paul rose and shielded his eyes again as he looked up and then down the beach. His legs nearly gave out and he stumbled back to sit heavily next to the mangroves. She tried walking but he could see her legs shaking before she sat back in the shade, her back to him.

"I'm so thirsty!" she cried.

Paul took off his shirt and tossed it to her. He picked up her shoe again. When he returned with the shoe, she was in his shirt, which barely covered her panties. She hurriedly covered her legs with the remains of her dress and drank the water greedily.

"What are we going to do?" she said, her eyes finally looking into Paul's. "I can't stay out in the sun like this." She showed him her arms. "My skin is like porcelain."

Rising again, Paul stepped back through the mangroves to the large black plants with leaves the size of elephant ears. It took nine trips to gather enough leaves. He had a harder time getting through the mangrove vines. Paul found a line of wild bamboo and used a rock to cut enough stalks down.

It was late afternoon by the time Paul finished building the lean-to, with an elephant-leaf roof and bamboo support poles, all tied together with mangrove vines. He used the rest of the elephant leaves for a soft floor.

"Good," she said as she came in and sat, carefully covering her legs with her torn dress, lest he see her panties again. "Now what about food?"

Paul had already thought of that and picked up the last bamboo shaft. He went back to the stream. After plunging his face into the water and drinking his fill again, he wetted the end of the bamboo and rubbed it against a rock. It took a while to sharpen the stalk.

Passing the lean-to on his way back to the beach, Paul glanced in at her. She let out a long sigh and asked again, "What about food?"

"I'm working on it," he said. "Why don't you start a fire?"

"A fire? How?"

"You rub sticks together."

When he looked back, he could see she wasn't budging.

Paul walked to a series of small rocks. Using them as stepping stones, he moved to the farthest rock and tried spear-fishing. He missed three fish before accidentally rousting a huge lobster, which he promptly speared.

He impaled three more lobsters before heading back to the lean-to.

"Are you sure no one else made it to this island?" she asked.

"No."

"Did you search, at least?"

Paul shook his head and she looked away before he could explain the obvious, he'd been busy building the lean-to and getting food.

As the red sun sank into the distant sky, streaking the sea in a purple glow, Paul started a fire. He saw her peeking at him from the lean-to as he began cooking the lobsters. He would have preferred boiling the lobsters, but the broiled lobster tails were delicious.

While they ate, Paul found the courage to ask her name.

"Please!" she said in that same dismissive voice pretty girls always seem to use. He knew he was ugly. She didn't have to remind him. His jaw was too big and the protruding brow on his forehead gave him the nickname he hated through high school – 'Link' (as in missing link).

When they finished, she announced she had to go to the bathroom. She stepped from the lean-to and said, "If I catch you watching me, I'll tell the authorities when we're rescued."

As if I want to watch someone going to the bathroom.

Paul stepped around the other side of the lean-to and carried a large rock back to the fire. He dropped it in the center of the burning driftwood, sending sparks into the air, then sat and began using the rock to fire-sharpen his spear.

When she came back, she sat across the fire, draping her torn dress across her legs. She watched him for a while before stating, suspiciously, "I didn't see you on the yacht."

"I was the assistant cook."

She looked out at the dark sea. "When do you think we'll be rescued?"

"The automatic distress call should have gone out when the boat started to break up."

"I can't believe this," she said, got up and went into the lean-to. A moment later, she called out, "I hope you don't think you're sleeping in here with me."

Paul slept under the bright stars of Octavion's moonless sky, the soothing sounds of the waves rolling to shore, the mangroves shifting in the sea breeze flowing over the island.

•••

Pterodactyls woke Paul at dawn, with their loud screeching as they dove into the surf. Paul watched the pesky, little bastards fight over their catches, darting and diving, slashing at each other with their claws.

Standing and stretching, Paul peeked in the lean-to. She lay on her back, with head toward him. She was so pretty, Paul felt his heart immediately race as he traced her face, the line of her sculptured lips.

Moving into the mangroves, Paul searched until he found the gray-green seed pods he'd seen the previous day on his hurried trips to the spring. He brought the pods to the stream and cracked them on a boulder. It took several trips before he succeeded in cracking them correctly, before he could carry four pods full of water back to the lean-to.

He carefully dug holes in the sand to prop-up the pods and keep from spilling the water before taking his fire-sharpened spear back to the rocks. The pterodactyls had driven fish to the rocks and Paul managed to spear two large sea salmons.

He used a boulder to smash several smaller rocks until one shattered lengthwise. He picked up the broken stone and used the sharpened edge to scale and gut the fish. He was 'Link', a missing link, living back in the stone-age, using rocks for tools.

The sizzling smell of the fish made Paul's stomach rumble as he sat next to the fire. He saw her stir, then sit up.

"That smells great." she said as she rose and brushed down Paul's shirt.

"Thanks."

"I didn't say you smelled great. Whatever you're cooking … Oh, forget it." She walked off into the mangroves. Paul watched her move away, half of her panties sticking out of his shirt.

When she returned she was careful to point her legs away from Paul as she sat and devoured her fish. She drank two of the water pods, then rose and said she was going to bathe in the surf.

"I catch you peeking at me and I'll claw your eyes out when you're sleeping."

She called back over her shoulder as she moved away. "Why don't you go get us some greens in the forest? We can't eat fish and lobsters all the time."

Maybe you can't.

Paul went into the woods, as far away from the bathing woman as he could get. He wasn't good enough to even see her naked. Not him. And for the thousandth time, he was back in high school, averting his eyes when a pretty girl spoke to him.

• • •

In the evening, after refilling the water pods, Paul took his spear back to the rocks and immediately speared a huge, green Sea bass that took all his strength to land. He dragged it off the rocks and up the beach before returning for his spear.

As he set his feet and lifted his spear, an entire school of fish suddenly surged against the rocks. Before he could spear one, fish began flopping up on the rocks. Dropping his spear, Paul used both hands to grab a fish and toss it up on the beach. Another wave brought more fish and Paul tossed another and another.

The sea broke over his feet and he stopped, realizing the water was surging up. He spotted a large wave rolling toward him and leaped off the other side of the rocks and started wading to shore. The wave broke over the rocks and a mammoth head shot out of the water, its hideous mouth filled with fish.

Elasmosaur.

Paul raced through knee-deep water to the beach.

The elasmosaur's head tilted back and shook as it swallowed its catch.

Paul hit the beach at a full run and didn't look back until he reached the mangroves. The elasmosaur continued its feeding frenzy, its long neck twisting as it gobbling mouthfuls of fish.

Jogging next to the mangroves, Paul reached the lean-to just as she peeked out.

"What's all the commotion?"

He pointed to the sea.

She let out a cry. "What's that!?"

"Elasmosaur." Paul sat outside the lean-to, pulling his knees up to his chest. "That's why we had the guns on the yacht."

"What guns?"

Paul didn't bother explaining about the 20mm cannons.

"Will it come out of the water?"

"I hope not."

"You know," she huffed, "you're not very encouraging."

A half hour after the hideous beast's head disappeared back into the sea, Paul cautiously went for the sea bass and the other fish he'd left on the beach. He found several others, flopping on the sand.

The bass was so delicious, Paul ate too much. She did too and complained that she was probably going to gain weight at this rate.

Just as the sun disappeared along the eastern horizon, a driving rain storm blew in from the sea. Easing into the mangroves, Paul watched the rain put out their fire, sending a white cloud into the dark sky. The cool, rain-swept breeze felt good on his face and the island smelled of wet leaves when the fast moving storm was over.

Paul re-started the fire immediately. She peeked out of the lean-to a few minutes later, raised a hand to check if it was still raining, then came to sit by the fire.

"That was some rainstorm," Paul said, stoking the fire with his newest bamboo spear. He sharpened it against the rock.

She pulled her long blonde hair away from her face and jutted her jaw toward the water.

"Where are the rescuers?"

Paul just shrugged.

She pointed at the sea. "I thought I saw something earlier. Is there land out there?"

"When I was on top the hill, I didn't see any land."

She let out a long sigh and stretched her legs, carefully covering her crotch with her hand. "Glad you didn't try coming in the lean-to during the rain. I could barely breath in there."

Standing, she yawned and stretched, then caught herself and tugged Paul's shirt down to nearly cover her panties.

"What you should do is build a shelter for yourself." She went into her lean-to and lay with her head pointing his way.

Paul watched the sea roll to shore, the water shimmering in the starlight, and eventually lay on his back between the fire and the lean-to, his feet toward to the sea, his arms behind his head. His steady breathing lulled him to sleep and he dreamed …

… she stood at the water's edge with her back to him as he sat by the fire. She shook out her long, golden hair and ran her fingers through it. Then, slowly, she pulled the shirt over her head and let it fall. Twisting her head around, she smiled at him as she climbed out of her panties and walked into the surf.

Paul followed her into the water and swam with her under the stars.

She floated on her back, arms and legs spread as she lay in the water. Paul traced the curves of her body, lingering on her breasts and the silky mat between her legs.

He followed her again, out of the water to lie on their backs on the beach. He watched her chest rise and fall with her steady breathing, her eyes closed as she lay next to him.

Moving his head over hers, he hesitated before softly kissing her lips. Her hand moved behind his head and pulled at his hair as their tongues worked against each other's.

She let out little gasping cries as they made love on the beach …

Paul woke with a jerk and sat up.

It took a while for him to catch his breath.

The ache in his chest was numbing. It was a mystery why he felt so, every time he looked at her, an even greater mystery than why creatures on Octavion were so much like the dinosaurs of Earth, a mystery scientists were unable to solve.

The conflict of the human heart.

Paul's heartache continued as he tired to go back to sleep.

• • •

It wasn't the pterodactyl's noise that woke Paul the next morning. Groggily, he realized he had been listening to the pesky bastards when they went suddenly quiet. In the dim, morning light,

Paul watched something moving out into the sea, just this side of the rocks. It was little more than a shadow, as it stood on its hind legs looking around at the water. Slowly, it turned and walked steadily toward the mangroves, its long tail swishing from side to side as it moved, slowly, confidently. Reaching the mangroves, the beast stopped and looked around.

As a breath of sea air blew over Paul, he realized they were thankfully downwind from the beast. And as the dawn slowly brightened, he recognized the it – *raptor*, standing at least five feet tall. Dark green with an orange belly, the raptor twisted its head around in jerky movements, like a bird.

Paul felt his heart pounding as the beast started moving their way.

The loud squeal of a pterodactyl turned the raptor's gaze back to the sea as the pterodactyls went at it again.

"What is that racket?" Her voice boomed from the lean-to, snapping the raptor's head their way.

Paul inched his hand for the new, fire-hardened spear, lying next to his feet.

"Damn those things," she said as she came out and stood next to Paul.

The raptor darted forward.

Paul jumped to his feet, brandishing his spear.

"Get into the mangroves," he said. "Get up in a tree!"

"What? Are you insane?"

The raptor closed quickly as Paul tossed extra driftwood onto the fire, stoking it with his spear.

"What's that!?"

"Raptor," he answered. "Now get into the mangroves and up into a tree." She let out a high-pitched moan and Paul heard her hurried footsteps moving away from him.

The raptor slowed as it closed in. Paul stepped behind the fire. Twisting its head in jerks, it seemed confused by the human form. It sniffed the air. Suddenly its eyes narrowed and it let out a screech and ran straight at Paul, circling the fire so quickly, Paul barely had time to lift the spear.

141

The raptor crashed against the spear, sending Paul to the sand.

It screeched and tumbled past Paul, the spear imbedded in its side.

Paul grabbed his last spear and crawled around the fire again.

Jumping to its clawed feet, the raptor slapped the spear from its side and stared at its wound for a moment before letting out a more piercing, chilling screech. It lowered its head and crept forward.

Paul picked up a burning log of driftwood with his left hand and held it in front of him as the two circled the fire. The raptor's side was streaked in red now. Paul fought to keep the fire's smoke from burning his eyes. He swung his torch menacingly, as they continued circling the fire. The raptor bared its curved teeth and snapped its jaws.

The raptor stopped and began backing away. It lowered its head even further as Paul dropped his torch and held the spear with two shaking hands. He crept closer to the fire. Suddenly, the beast leaped high, over the fire, talons slashing as it came down. Paul raised his spear.

The raptor crashed straight down on the bamboo spear, snapping it as its talons caught Paul's side. Tumbling past Paul, the raptor's scream drowned out Paul's screaming. His side burning, Paul managed to grab the torch and wheel.

The raptor lay writhing on its back, legs kicking, arms flailing, the broken spear had impaled it completely. Paul leaped for it, shoving the torch into his eye. The beast howled and Paul ground the torch into the other eye.

It snapped its hideous jaws and tried to slash Paul with its razored-talons. Paul shoved the still burning torch into the raptor's mouth and held on as it strangled. The strength in his arms gave way and Paul staggered back toward the fire. Falling straight back, he managed to press his hands against his bleeding side. He didn't want to pass out but felt his head swim.

Closing his eyes, he struggled to keep breathing, the burning on his sides giving way to a deep, shattering pain. His breath shortened and he concentrated on the pain to keep him awake. The crackling of the fire slowly ebbed and the sound of the surf became more pronounced. The pain didn't subside one bit, coming in waves with each breath.

• • •

The bright sun beat through his closed eyelids and he pressed them even tighter until he felt a movement next to him in the sand. Blinking his eyes open, he saw her standing above him, long blonde hair hanging alongside that beautiful face.

She lifted her head and looked away out at the sea and began yelling.

Struggling, Paul tried lifting his head, but there was no strength left. He sucked in deeply, the pain stabbing him and with all his strength, pushed himself up on one elbow. He was covered in blood from his chest down.

He looked over at the raptor and it was lying still.

She bounced next to him. Waving her arms frantically, she yelled again. Paul wasn't sure, but he thought he saw something in the water. A boat. White and orange. *Coast Guardsmen.*

Slowly Paul sank back. The pain was subsiding. He felt a sudden chill.

Suddenly she was there, hovering over him, speaking to him as never before, in a voice so soft he couldn't hear what she said. He stared up into those eyes as blue as the Cerulean Sea. She smiled and craned her face forward, pursing her lips. She closed her eyes as their lips touched.

Paul couldn't feel his legs anymore. And the pain was gone as she pulled her lips away.

The beautiful eyes were filled with tears.

She spoke again but he couldn't hear.

She's telling me she's sorry. She feels it now. Finally.

Her hair brushed the side of his face as she leaned forward and pressed her lips against his again.

• • •

The young coast guardsman watched the blonde woman waving frantically as she stood next to the fire that had caught their attention. As their craft eased up on the beach, he jumped out and jogged to the woman. She continued waving and as he closed in, could see she wore a striped shirt and white panties that were too sheer. Even with her hair messed, she was very pretty.

It was then he saw the bloody man lying on the far side of the fire. Looking around, he spotted the raptor, pulled out his pistol and walked over to the beast.

Dead.

The woman was crying now and grinning at the same time.

The young coast guardsman holstered his weapon and went down on his knees next to the bloody man. His side had been sliced open. He checked for a pulse.

Standing he asked the woman, "Who was he?"

"I don't know. A cook on our yacht." She batted her eyes at him and smiled.

"He's dead," he said.

"Dead?" She seemed surprised. "But he was kissing the air a minute ago."

THE END *of* "Were Yellow as Gold"

Predator of the Spearmint Forest

The vast Spearmint Forest, with its bright green trees and turquoise leaves, occupied most of the northern hemisphere of planet Octavion, from the multi-colored waters of the Painted Ocean to the pale green Jade Sea and brilliant blue Sapphire Sea. Mostly unexplored, the Spearmint Forest, unlike much of Octavion, had no known predators, until after the humans came.

As their land rover parked at the edge of the forest, Dana looked at the forest's bright green tree trunks, at the leaves shimmering gold in the afternoon sunlight, then looked beyond the trees at the spooky darkness of the deep forest.

"This is it," said her father, turning off the engine.

From the backseat, Dana's cousin Tallie looked around and said, "Looks scary to me." Dana and Tallie were both thirteen, Dana the adventurous one, Tallie the talker.

"The only bad thing that can happen to you in the Spearmint Forest," Dad said, "is if you get lost and you won't get lost because you're not going anywhere without me." He was looking at Dana now because she'd gotten lost before. She gave him a knowing smile as they all climbed out of the rover.

"We have about two hours until sunset, so let's get started." Dad lifted the rear hatch of the rover, leaving it up to attach the tent and began pulling out the gear. The girls helped, Dana tuning out Tallie as she yakked about the tent, the coolers, the lamps, the sleeping bags for each girl inside the rover, the cot her father would sleep on outside in the tent that extended from the rear of the rover for a good twenty feet.

"You going to shoot something?" Tallie noticed the rifle.

"It shoots tranquilizer darts." Dad showed the girls the small darts with bright orange feathers. Then he showed them the special infrared lights and night-vision goggles, one for each of them.

"I told you this would be a working vacation," he said as he set up his cot.

"We're here now," said Dana. "So you can tell us the secret."

Dad nodded and explained as he continued setting up the gear, "There is a predator around here, not dangerous to people, but very dangerous to the small forest animals. We're here to capture it."

He pulled a wire contraption and popped it open into a cage and placed it on a table.

"What kind of predator?" Dana asked impatiently.

Dad smiled. "I need you two to help me catch it."

Tallie gave inquisitive look and asked, "How do you know it can't hurt people?"

"Because it's small. Four or five pounds and if it's what we think it is, it won't hurt you unless you grab it with our hands." Dad stood and stretched. In his khaki ranger uniform, he looked more like a solider than an environmental policeman. "That's why I brought the tranquilizer gun."

He pulled the water cooler to the rear edge of the rover and poured three cups of cool water, passing them around.

Tallie finished hers first and said, "So, what are we doing tonight? I brought three movies."

Dad shook his head.

Dana moaned at her father, "You're not going to tell us camp fire stories, are you?"

"No." He lifted the night-vision goggles. "We're going hunting tonight. When it's dark enough. This predator is a nocturnal hunter."

Dana looked at the dark forest. "In there?"

"Of course."

Tallie let out a mousey squeal and Dad laughed.

• • •

They lay on a patch of sweet smelling grass on a small knoll between two trees, not far from a stand of coral-leafed burgundy bushes and several clumps of prickly greenish-yellow chartreuse bushes that looked fluorescent in the night-vision goggles. Earlier, when it was still daylight, Dana helped her Dad set up the special infra-red lights around the area. He turned them on after dark and when they put on the goggles, it looked like daylight even though it was pitch black. The infra-red light was invisible, except through the goggles.

Dana, her father and Tallie lay on their bellies, all three watching the bushes, all silent because Dad said the slightest noise would scare away the predator and the small, scurrying animals it preyed upon.

Earlier, as they ate supper next to the fire her Dad had carefully lit in a clearing away from the tent and trees, Dana asked how they knew there was a predator at work.

"Our patrols found the bones of freshly killed animals with teeth marks that can only come from a predator."

Dana thought about it a moment before she said, "Could it have been a scavenger?"

"What's the difference?" Tallie asked as she looked beyond the fire at the dark forest.

"Scavengers eat animals after they die, like from injury or old age. Predators hunt animals."

Tallie shook her head. "I don't like this."

"You can stay in the rover, watch your movies. I'll lock you in, leave you the keys."

Tallie looked at Dana, then back at her uncle and said, "No. I'll stay. I guess."

By the time Dana spotted her first forest animal, Tallie was sleeping next to her. A mouse-sized Octavion striped lemur crept from the chartreuse bushes and began nibbling on seeds from the burgundy bushes.

Dana sucked in a breath of excitement and felt her Dad's hand on her shoulder as he let out a nearly silent, "Shush."

The lemur stood up on its rear legs, twisting its oversized ears around, then slowly went back to its nibbling. Another lemur joined it a few minutes later but remained closer to the thick chartreuse bushes.

At least the air was cool along the forest floor and smelled so fresh as Dana lay watching the small animals in their natural habitat and again wondered what type of predator was killing them. Her father was keeping the secret, wanting to surprise her she was sure. She was glad Tallie was asleep because Dana knew she'd make a noise when the predator appeared, if it did, and Dana was determined to not do that.

A movement to their left caught Dana's attention as a small rodent came from beneath other bushes. It began nibbling the burgundy seeds. The rodent had a long tail with a tuft of hair at the end and smaller ears than the lemur and was stouter. Surely, this wasn't the predator.

Dana spotted the predator an hour later and felt her father tense up. At first she wasn't sure what she was seeing – a wide, round face, pointy ears trained straight ahead, and owly eyes so wide and dark and unblinking as the cat sneaked out from a chartreuse bush. It froze in place as one of the lemurs stood up and looked around.

It was a ordinary house *cat,* striped, a tabby. Dana knew all about cats, had a big book of cats and several movies she'd watched over and over again. She'd even visited cats in the zoo and played with the kittens, the cutest animals she'd ever seen. But cats were banned as pets on Octavion because, like this one, they got away and wrecked havoc on the defenseless creatures who knew nothing of such predators.

Dana realized she was holding her breath and let it out slowly, feeling her Dad moving next to her. She glanced over and saw he was carefully bringing the rifle up into position.

She looked back at the cat, which hadn't moved. The lemurs and rodents, there were several now, had gone back to eating. Moving stealthily, the cat tip-toed closer, its wide eyes locked on its prey. It froze again and waited. As one of the lemurs moved, Dana could see the cat's eyes following it, although the feline remained motionless. The lemur bent to pick up another seed and the cat crept closer, hunkered down, its body as flat as it could make it, its rear paws stepping into the spot vacated by its front paws.

In a rush, the cat streaked past two lemurs and pounced on its prey, pinning a lemur down and biting the back of its neck. The lemur stopped moving and the cat looked up and around as the small animals scattered. Suddenly the lemur started moving again and the cat let it go. The lemur limped away and Dana saw the muzzle of her father's rifle inch forward.

She held her breath for one, two, three second waiting for the dart to fly. Instead she saw the muzzle lower and looked back as two kittens came rushing from the bushes and pounced on the wounded lemur. One fell off and swatted at the lemur with its paw as the mother cat sat watching, then began licking its paw.

The muzzle rose again as Dad took careful aim. Dana held her breath and saw the dart fly and strike the cat on the rump. The cat jumped and turned and bit at the orange feathers, bounced twice and fell. The kittens didn't notice their mother go down as they had the lemur cornered.

Dana watched her Dad slip on a pair of leather gloves and pull a net from the pouch on his belt. He rose slowly and crept forward, raising the net as he moved. One of the kittens bounced and swatted at the lemur again as the second bit it. The lemur stopped.

Her Dad got within throwing distance and tossed the net at the kittens. He caught the one biting the lemur, but the second kitten ran into the bush. By the time Dana got there, her father had reached under the net and had kitten in hand. He tossed the net aside and pulled a bag from his pouch.

The kitten hissed at Dana as she stepped up, still watching it through her night-vision goggles. It was so cute with its stripes and the way it hissed. Dad slipped the kitten into the bag and Dana saw the bag was a net bag. Pulling the tie-string to close the bag, Dad tied a quick knot and put the bag on the ground. The kitten hissed again, its little claws sticking through the bag's mesh now as Dad scooped up the dead lemur and moved over to the mother cat.

He gently lifted the cat, cradled it in his arms and pulled out the dart.

"Pick up the bag," her Dad told her. "Don't jiggle it too much."

Dana picked up the draw string and lifted the bag with the kitten that gave out a little howl.

"It's OK, kitty." Dana said, making sure she didn't swish the bag around too much as she followed her Dad back to where they'd left Tallie and the dart rifle. The kitty howled a little louder and Dana saw Tallie stirring.

"Wake up, sleepy-head," Dad said as he bent down to pick up his rifle.

Tallie lifted her head and said, "What'd I miss?"

Dana held up the bag and the kitty hissed again and Tallie let out a squeal.

"Come on." Dad led them back to their camp.

"What about the other kitten?" Dana asked as Tallie trailed next to her, Tallie still staring at the captured kitten who had its legs extended as it rocked in the moving bag.

"What other kitten?" asked Toni.

"If you going to sleep through things," Dana said. "You're going to miss a lot."

Stepping into the tent, everyone pulled off their goggles and Dad turned on the lights. Dana blinked and it took a minute for her to see clearly. She watched her Dad place the cat on the table. Then he took the bag from Dana, reached in and the kitten tried to swat him, managing to bite the thick glove before her Dad pulled it out. He held it up by the nape of its neck for the girls to take a closer look.

"Doesn't that hurt?" Tallie asked.

Dana answered, "No. It's the way the mother carries it."

"Huh?"

"They don't have hands."

Tallie rolled her eyes.

The kitten stared back at Dana and looked around, looking so tiny and fragile. In the bright light Dana saw the kitten was striped, gray and black. Tallie lifted a hand to pet the kitten which tried to swat her, only Dad pulled the kitten back.

"It's wild," he said as he put the kitten in the cage.

He pulled off his gloves and examined the cat. "I'm making sure she'd not injured. He checked her teeth and each paw. "She's in good shape."

"What happened to it?" Tallie asked.

"Tranquilized," Dad said before Dana could snap at her cousin.

"Tranquilized?"

Dana pointed to the rifle on the table. "Remember the dart gun?"

"Oh."

Dad brought out a hypodermic and withdrew a little blood from the cat's leg.

"What's that for?" Tallie asked.

"To make sure she doesn't have anything wrong with her," Dana answered for her Dad who nodded and pulled out another hypo and a medicine bottle, stuck the hypo in and pulled out some pink liquid into the hypo and gave the cat a shot.

"This medicine will wake her up."

IIe put the mother cat into the cage, the kitten jumping to the back of the cage as soon as he opened it, then went straight to its mother and nestled against her belly as she lay on her side. The mother's coat was darker but with the same mottled stripes. Dad put a bowl of water and bowl of dried food in the cage.

While he examined the dead lemur, Dana and Tallie watched the cat slowly wake. The kitten began to nurse and the cat lifted its head, looking straight at Dana. It didn't hiss or even snarl as it looked around the cage.

Later, when the kitten had finished nursing, the cat sat up and looked around again, the kitten pressed against her side.

"They're frightened," Dad said, "but their safe here with plenty food and water."

"What are you going to do with them?" Tallie asked.

"The zoo, right Dad?"

"That's right, Dana. They'll be well taken care of and they won't be killing native species anymore. They don't belong in the wild."

Dana gave that a thought for a moment before saying, "They are pretty good hunters, aren't they?"

151

"Felines are some of the most efficient predators. Saw how the mother only wounded its prey to let the kittens practice. She's teaching them how to hunt."

They pulled up chairs and watched the mother cat groom herself, then groom her kitten, licking it as the kitten nuzzled her. Then the cat let out a sharp yowl.

"She's calling her other kitty," said Dad.

"Other kitty?" Tallie asked and Dana slapped her own forehead.

"The one that got away."

Tallie seemed to think a moment before coming back with, "It'll starve without its mother."

Dad stretched and said, "Its hiding right now but we'll get it in the morning."

"How?" Tallie asked and Dana wanted to know too.

Dad turned down the lights and went over to his cot, sat and took off his boots. He smiled back at the girls and said, "Don't stay up too late."

• • •

In the morning, Dana woke to a scratching sound. She climbed out of the rover and spotted the kitten climbing inside the cage, its claws scraping against the metal rungs. The kitten froze when Dana got close and went, "Meow."

Dana stuck her finger in the cage and brushed the kitten's long tail. The kitten, hanging on to the cage, hissed.

"Oh, shush," Dana said, pulling up a chair. "You're not a tiger. You're just a kitty."

The mother cat, which was napping, lifted its head and let out a low growl which sent Dana tumbling back off her chair and woke up her Dad, who laughed as he got up.

"Good, they ate all the food," he said before refilling the food dish, using a long tube so he didn't have to put his hand in the cage. He refilled the water dish too, then started on their breakfasts. Dana sat back on her chair and watched the cats, who just sat there watching her.

Over breakfast, with sleepy-eyed Tallie barely there, Dad explained how all domestic cats were directly descended from the wild cats of Africa. "Back on Earth, cats are the top predators in many places, especially Africa. Beside the big cats – lions, leopards and cheetahs – there are caracals, servals, and the wild cats, smaller than most domestic cat breeds. That's why we can't let felines loose here. They'll unbalance the environment.

Tallie yawned. "What about tigers?"

"They're from Asia."

Tallie looked confused as usual.

"Earth. Earth. Earth," she complained. "That's all we talk about sometimes."

Dana's Dad opened his mouth but before he could say it, Dana said, "If we don't know where we came from we won't know where wc're going."

Tallie looked even more confused.

After a good breakfast, Dad led them back to where they'd set up the night before. Dana and Tallie watched with fascination as he spread a wide net between several trees, then raised the net about five feet from the ground. He placed the cage with the cat and kitten on the forest floor below the net before he made the girls move away with him to hide.

"What are we doing?" Tallie asked, ever confused.

Dad whispered, "The missing kitten will be very hungry now. Its hiding place can't be far away. The kitten will come out hesitantly and call for its mother and she'll call back. It'll come close and we'll drop the net on it.

"Doesn't the mother see it's a trap?" asked Toni.

Dana rolled her eyes at her cousin.

"Not really. Cats don't think like we do. The mother will call back because it's her nature. She's a good mother."

Tallie said, "A good mother would tell it to keep hiding."

Dana smiled at her Dad.

Lying again on the soft blue grass, partially hidden from the cage by a huge spearmint tree, Dana watched dapple sunlight play off the turquoise leaves. A breeze filtering through the forest felt cool, even as the strong Octavion sun climbed in the sky. Birds began to flit around, long-tailed bluebirds and pale green thrushes with their even longer tails and nearly a dozen orange doves gathered on the ground to eat the berries and seeds from the trees and bushes.

Dana kept a wary eye out for the red killer-shrike, the bright crimson bird with it long yellow beak. Shrikes survived on eating the chicks of other birds while they were away from their nests. The minutes drew into an hour and longer.

Tallie inched close to her uncle and whispered, loud enough for Dana to hear, "Why don't you use the dart gun when the kitten comes out?"

Dad explained patiently, "Too small to hit and the tranquilizer might kill it."

Tallie nodded, then yawned.

A bird Dana had never seen before landed three feet away on a burgundy bush. It chirped and picked at a berry with its small beak. The bird was blue-purple and small, plump and looked – fluffy. It fluttered away with the berry.

"That's a periwinkle bunting," Dad whispered.

Dana nodded as Tallie yawned again.

"This is boring." Tallie said a little too loud, scattering several doves.

So Dad said he'd take Tallie back to the camp, so she could entertain herself with a movie inside the rover.

"If anyone shows up or any dinosaur comes along, just blow the horn and we'll come save you."

Even Tallie knew that was a joke.

Dad handed Dana the control switch for the net, telling her if the kitten came close to the cage to press the red button and the net would fall.

"I'll be right back."

They were just out of sight when Dana heard a kitten cry out. She inched forward and saw the cat and kitten in the cage both standing and staring across the clearing. She heard the cry again and realized it was the kitten in the cage.

The mother let out a sharp cry which was immediately answered. But the answer didn't come from the kitten in the cage, it came from the distant bushes. Dana felt her heart beating faster and looked back for her Dad but he was gone.

Turning back, she saw the kitten come out of the bushes. It stood up in the grass and let out a long cry, answered immediately by its mother. The kitten took a hesitant step forward, then crouched, lowering its ears as it crept toward the cage.

The mother let out a sharper cry and the kitten cried back then stopped. Dana's finger itched on the button, but the kitten wasn't under the net yet. A large orange dove landed near the kitten, oblivious to the fact a predator was closely, albeit a small predator, and began pecking for seeds. The kitten stood frozen and stared at the bird for a long moment, then bounded back to the bushes.

Dana let out her breath and pulled her finger from the switch when the kitten suddenly came from the other side of the bush and raced for its mother. Dana pushed the button. Nothing. She pushed it again but nothing happened.

The kitten stopped just outside the cage and let out a long, "Meow."

The mother called back with a sharp, "Meow."

Dana waited for the remote to re-cycle. The kitten took a step backward and Dana eased the button down. The net seemed to float for a moment, then came down quickly, covering the kitten, the cage and the dove.

Dana stood up and shouted for her father.

"Right here," he called back and stepped through the trees. "I was watching. You did well." He pulled on his gloves, went around and let the dove out, then carefully worked the net to get the kitten which was so shocked all it did was blink its eyes at him.

"Is it hurt?" Dana asked.

"Surprised is a better words. And very hungry. He tilted the cage on its side, putting the mother and other kitty off balance, opened the door and put the new kitten inside before slowly turning the cage back upright.

While he gathered the net and the infra-red lights, Dana watched the mother cat lick her missing kitty as it nursed. The first kitten seemed just as curious of Dana as she was of them and stared at her with its yellow eyes.

• • •

"Did I miss anything?" Tallie asked when they returned to camp.

Dad put the cage back on the table.

"They're twins," Dana said as Tallie rushed over to look at the new kitten and Dad refilled the food and water dishes before he started to break camp.

"Go ahead and watch the kittens," he told Dana when she started to help pack up. "I'll get the gear."

So Dana and Tallie watched the kittens play with one another as the mother cat lay at the far side of the cage and kept a wary eye on the two girls watching them. All of the cats had bright yellow eyes and the kitten's tails stood straight up as they darted back and forth, pouncing on one another and letting out little "Meows."

Once the second kitten had stopped nursing, Dana couldn't tell them apart. She tried hard but couldn't.

"So what are you going to name them?" Dad said as he stepped back up.

"We get to name them?"

"Sure. They'll need to be called something at the zoo and you found them."

The girls looked back at the felines.

Tallie declared, "The kittens are Annie and Brandy."

"You don't get to name both," Dana argued.

"OK. I'll name that one Annie," Tallie pointed to the kitten who was licking its paw.

"The other one will be Eleanor," said Dana.

"Actually," Dad said. "Eleanor should be the mother's name because I get to name one and you can't call the kittens Annie or Eleanor."

"Why not."

"They're males."

Tallie made a face and Dana immediately said, "Mine's name is David."

"I wanted that name," Tallie argued.

"OK," said Dana, "Call yours David and I'll call mine Devin."

Tallie agree and that was how Dana got to name all the cats.

The cat cage was the last item to go into the back of the rover. Dad put it close to the back seat so the girls could watch the cats.

"This was a complete success," Dana declared as they pulled away from the camp site.

"Almost," said Dad.

"What else is there to do?"

"There's another predator out there."

"There is?"

"Think about it. We have a mother and kittens …"

"The father," Dana said sharply, causing Tallie to jump.

Dad looked back at the Spearmint Forest as they drove away and said, "Finding the more elusive tom cat won't be so easy."

"Good. I can't wait!" said Dana.

"I'll pass on that one," said Tallie as the mother cat let out a loud hiss, making Tallie pull her hand away.

"Leave them alone," Dana told her cousin.

Dad smiled in the rearview mirror.

"That cat gets a hold of one of your fingers, you'll see why she's a top predator."

The girls remained content to just watch the mother cat and her kitten all the way back to Bronze Town.

THE END *of* **"Predator of the Spearmint Forest"**

for my daughter Dana

A Frightful Fiend

And having once turned round walks on,
And turns no more his head;
Because he knows, a frightful fiend
Doth close behind him tread.

"The Rime of the Ancient Mariner"
Samuel Taylor Coleridge (Earth, 1798 a.d.)

"Mr. Garrick will be with you presently."

The old butler bows slightly, turns and leaves Jonas Park standing just inside the doorway of the dark, paneled room.

Park watches the old man walk back down the long hall. Thin and hunched, wearing a black tuxedo and patent leather shoes, the white-haired butler moves away slowly. In his fifty years, Park never met a real butler before. It is an unexpected luxury in the wild, western hemisphere of such a distant planet as Octavion.

Park waits until the man-servant disappears around a far corner in the hall, turns and steps into the paneled room. He stops immediately and pulls off his jungle hat. At an even six-feet tall, Park is a barrel-chested man with a craggy face, weathered from years under the strong Octavion sun. His sky-blue eyes stand out in stark contrast beneath thick reddish-brown eyebrows.

Wearing proper jungle attire – short-sleeve camouflaged shirt, matching fatigue pants and jungle boots of brown leather and canvass – Park stares straight ahead at a glass wall. He runs his left hand through thick, reddish-brown hair that is graying around the temples.

Beyond the glass wall, the wide Cerulean Sea glimmers in the fading sunlight. The evening sky, turning scarlet now, warms the paneled room in a dusty, orange glow. Park crosses the room to the glass wall and watches the bright blue water roll to the rocks below. The sea is streaked with splotches of purple and green and turquoise water. Tranquil, the Cerulean Sea is majestic in the waning light.

Looking at his feet, Park notices he's standing at the edge of a thick rug. The hardwood floor, exposed beyond the edge of the rug is dark. Probably from the Sepia Forest, Park figures. He notices a lamp to his right, next to an easy chair, and turns it on. He sees the color of the wall paneling now, redwood, probably from the Magenta Forest.

"So that's what I smell," he says aloud, as if the magenta wood can understand its rosy scent is pleasant to the human nose.

Turning around, Park lets out a long breath and stumbles back into the easy chair. He blinks, closes his eyes for a long moment, then opens them again.

Behind a large magenta wood desk, along the far wall, hangs two massive heads. On the right, the head of a pentaceratops is mounted. Its three horns, much longer than its better known cousin, triceratops, look sharp and menacing. The pentaceratops head is crowned by a large, spiked crown meant to protect its neck.

Park's gaze moves to the other mounted head. He lets out a high-pitched whistle. The head of an adult tyrannosaur dominates the wall. Its huge jaws open, the supreme land predator of the galaxy hangs in silent ferocity.

Standing, Park leaves his hat and moves across the room, around the desk to the tyrannosaur head. The enormous head measures at least five feet. Its dagger teeth, some more than seven inches long, line the colossal jaws. Park reaches up and runs his fingers along the inner edge of one tooth. Serrated, like a butcher's heavy chopping knife, the tooth is a perfect ripping tool.

"Wow!" Park's harsh whisper echoes in the room.

As he backs away, he hears footsteps behind him and turns as a tall, muscular man enters the room. Stopping momentarily, the man waits impatiently for Park to move out of the way so he can step around behind the desk.

At forty, Jon Garrick has an athlete's build, dark brown hair and a full beard. Also well-tanned, his dark eyes look at his watch as he sits in the high-backed chair behind his desk. Dressed in khakis, Garrick's hunting shirt has the standard-issue four pockets of the old-Earth safari hunter.

"All right, Mr. Park. You have five minutes."

Park nods toward the tyrannosaur. "That's an incredible trophy."

"Yes. Yes." Garrick waves a hand at the tyrannosaur head behind him. "My grandfather bagged it, back in the good ole days."

Park nods and looks around for a chair, realizing the only other chair is the easy chair across the room.

"Come on, man." Garrick thumps his fingers on his desk. "Your note said something about the greatest hunt."

Folding his arms, Park looks at the tyrannosaur again.

"No," Garrick moans. "You're not trying to sell me a secret way to hunt tyrannosaurs, are you?"

Still staring at the great beast, Park shakes his head.

"I'm not risking a twenty year sentence." Garrick looks back at the tyrannosaur for a moment. "Damn Indigenous Creature Act!"

Nodding, Park adds, "What a great time it must have been, back in the wild days, back when this dinosaur-infested planet was a hunter's paradise. Before the damn scientists started fussing about how they should be protected. All that research bunk, comparing our dinosaurs to Earth fossils."

"Nice speech," Garrick thumbs his fingers again on his desk. "You're down to three minutes."

Looking at the tyrannosaur, Park says, "Can you imagine the thrill hunting the ultimate predator?"

Garrick leans forward. "I've imagined it. More times than you could imagine. But what has that to do with us, now?"

"I know. Damn Indigenous Creature Act. Damn animals have all the rights today, including the right of way. Run into a pterodactyl with a hovercraft and you're fined the cost of a house. Shoot one and you –"

"I know the law!" Garrick stands. "Your time's up."

Park looks at his watch. "I still have a minute."

"What?"

Park reaches into the right pocket of his jungle shirt and pulls out a glass jar with a black cap. Stepping forward, he places the jar on the desk and watches Garrick lean down to look.

"Meet the most formidable predator in the known universe."

Garrick looks up at Park. "An ant?"

"Not just an *ant*. A Ponerine warrior ant. From our own mother Earth."

Garrick reaches under the desk and pushes something.

"My butler will show you out."

Park leans down and taps the jar. The dark brown ant scurries, its antennae tapping against the glass, its oversized head moving from side to side as it opens its jaws, then snaps them shut.

Park looks up. "You've heard of the miniaturization breakthrough, haven't you?"

Garrick stands and looks impatiently at the doorway.

"Well," Park says, "Have you?"

"What are you talking about?"

Park leans both hands on the desk and tells Garrick, in the simplest terms about the miniaturization discovery that is on the verge of revolutionizing inter-planetary travel.

"It's the greatest breakthrough since the Space Jump. We can miniaturize anything now. Even people."

He sees a hint of recognition in Garrick's eyes. Slowly, Garrick sits and looks at the glass wall.

"Yes. There was something in the news."

The butler arrives in the doorway and clears his throat.

Garrick adds, "I thought the technology wasn't perfected yet."

Park reaches into his left pocket and pulls out another jar. He places it on the desk. Garrick leans forward again and stares at an inch long horse in the jar.

"Sir?" the butler says.

Garrick looks at him and waves him away. As the butler turns to leave, Garrick says, "Bring us Bourbon. And ice."

"Scotch, if it's not too much trouble," Park says.

"Fine. Fine." Garrick waves the butler away as he watches the miniature horse move around in its jar.

Garrick looks at the ant again. "Why not shrink a dinosaur? A tyrannosaur?"

Park shrugs. "Too well guarded. You know how militant the Conservation Corps is. Besides, how do you get a tyrannosaur to stand still in a miniaturization chamber?"

"Yes. Yes." Pointing at the ant, Garrick says, "So, what is your proposition?"

He's not too bright, is he? Park smiles at his unspoken question.

He pushes the ant's jar closer and Garrick moves his chin down to get a better look. And Park explains his proposition in the simplest terms.

"You see, we shrink you down to a quarter inch. The Ponerine warrior ant, at one and a half inches, becomes the ultimate quarry. I have a terrarium." Park's voice rises. "A jungle terrarium in which I place you and one Ponerine warrior ant. It's man against beast."

The ant taps its antennae against the glass, opens its jaws again and snaps them shut.

"They look like ice-tong," Park says.

"What?"

"On Earth. A long time age. Haven't you ever seen pictures of men moving block of ice with huge tongs?"

"Yes," Garrick agrees. "Ice-tongs." He leans even closer to the ant. "Why is this such a formidable quarry?"

Park pauses a moment for emphasis and taps the top of the jaw, which sends the ant scurrying again. "You see," Park says, "the Ponerine is carnivorous."

Garrick looks up, his mouth forming a little "O."

The butler steps back in with a silver tray, an ice bucket, two bottles and two glasses. Without a word, and while Garrick watches the ant, the butler mixes their drinks, nods to Park and leaves.

Park places the bourbon next to Garrick and takes a sip of his scotch. The ice-cool drink bites at his tongue and warms him all the way to his stomach.

Still watching the Ponerine, Garrick picks up his drink, downs half in one gulp and then says, "Now explain it all by me again."

Park grins. He always grins when they're hooked.

• • •

Standing outside the door of the warehouse where Jonas Park waits inside with his miniaturization machine and terrarium, Jon Garrick flips on the switch of the multi-chip recorder concealed in his canvass hunting belt and says, "I am outside the warehouse now. As documented earlier on this chip, an extensive background check on this Jonas Park reveals an impeccable lineage. A direct descendant of the first settlers, Jonas Park's great-grandfather was a founding father of First Colony City."

Garrick switches his Browning big game rifle from his left shoulder to his right, holding on to the strap with his hand. He readjusts the bandoleer belt that crosses his chest. The belt's six compartments hold a total of fifty rounds of 30-06 ammunition.

"As I stand here, in anticipation of a great hunt, I am thrilled. I can't put it any better. Thrilled!"

The camouflage paint Garrick so carefully applied to his nose and around his eyes feels tight. It's reassuring, however, just as his camouflaged fatigues and the solid weight of the Browning on his shoulder.

Garrick checks himself again, checks his hunting belt with its over-sized canteen, bowie knife in its black sheath, binoculars in its sheath, night-vision goggles in yet another sheath. He taps the two smaller sheaths, one holding a red flask of fire accelerant, the other containing a black flask filled with a colorless liquid – hydrocyanic acid – cyanide in its purest form. A good hunter comes prepared. You never know when you might need enough cyanide to fell a heard of tyrannosaurs.

Garrick taps his steel-toed jungle boot against the metal steps on his way up to the warehouse door.

"The next sound will be the door opening."

He opens the steel door and steps inside the dark warehouse. The door closes automatically behind him as he moves quickly across the bare floor toward the only light in the place.

Jonas Park, standing beneath two huge lights, waves at Garrick. To Park's left lies the long table with the jungle terrarium. To his right is the thirty foot square booth that houses his miniaturization machine.

"The place smells of rotting plants," Garrick tells his recorder.

"That's the jungle." Parks waves to his terrarium.

"It's hot in here, hotter than last night."

Park points to a smaller terrarium next to the large one. "The Ponerine is tropical. It needs to be acclimated to the atmosphere before I insert it." He waves Garrick forward. "Come watch."

Park, in a white lab coat and wearing rubber gloves, inserts a steel instrument into the smaller terrarium. The instrument, a long rod with a scoop, has a chunk of red meat in the scoop.

Garrick looks closer. The large, brown ant moves toward the scoop. Its antennae waving as it scurries forward, the ant rapidly climbs into the scoop and attacks the meat.

Park lifts the scoop, takes two steps to his left and climbs a small ladder. Leaning into the large terrarium, Park stretches to place the scoop down on the terrarium's jungle floor. Garrick moves around and watches the Ponerine devour the meat.

"Hungry, isn't it?"

Park nods. "A Ponerine is always hungry." He turns the scoop and the meat and ant slide off to the jungle floor.

"One Ponerine. One human." Park looks at Garrick as he withdraws the scoop. "Man against beast."

Garrick walks around the large terrarium. At least thirty yards long and ten yards wide, it would seem like miles to a man one quarter inch tall. Three quarters of the terrarium is thick jungle. Garrick notes the long plateau on the far side and the hills beyond that run all the way to the glass. Circling the terrarium completely, he asks Park, "Where will I be deposited?"

"Same place I deposited the meat."

Garrick looks at the ground where the ant and meat were deposited.

"Where did it go?"

"Into the bush."

Garrick memorizes the trees and the layout of the small clearing, noting the quickest way to the plateau and hills.

"It's time to start," Park says.

"Fine."

Park leads the way to the miniaturization booth, turns and opens his mouth to ask a question.

"I've got the money right here," Garrick says, reaching into this top pocket and pulling out two thick bands of cash.

Park smiles, takes the money and says, "I was going to ask if I may see your weapon?"

"Sure." Garrick un-slings the Browning and passes it to Park who runs a hand over the glossy, walnut stock.

"Twentieth Century Earth," Garrick explains. "A big game gun. African Safaris. Used to kill elephants with one shot."

Park lifts the rifle, aims it across the warehouse, then hands it back to Garrick. Patting the bandoleer, he says, "Brought enough ammo?"

"Fifty rounds."

"You'll need them." Park flashes a cold smile.

Garrick shoulders the weapon and says, "Let's get started."

Park leads Garrick into the white chamber, to a small stainless-steel chair beneath a crystal dome. Park reminds him to remain still and walks out, closing the door behind him.

"Park warned of the nausea but it isn't so bad," Garrick tells his recorder.

As instructed, Garrick keeps his eyes closed as the dizzying effects of miniaturization overtake him. It is quickly followed by the sensation of rapid movement and then the stomach flipping feeling of an elevator dropping quickly.

Finally, Garrick feels a warm light on his face and a stale breath of air brushes across him. He opens his eyes to a bright green world of chirping birds and buzzing insects. Looking up he shades his eyes from the artificial sun above and smiles.

"I have to hand it to Park, this is . . . incredible."

Standing, Garrick checks his watch and notes the time. He stretches as he takes in a deep whiff of chlorophyll-scented air.

Unslinging his rifle, he looks carefully at the foliage. He recognizes two large trees to his right, and moves toward them, knowing that is the way to the plateau.

"I hear birds, but cannot see any. I wonder if the sounds are artificial."

Stopping by a tree, he pulls off a leaf and breaks it.

"The plants are real enough, so that means the insect sounds are real."

A dragonfly floats past Garrick's nose.

"I'm impressed. The meticulous work keeping this jungle going is incredible. Insects to pollinate. Amazing."

Scanning the brush, he ducks and moves between the trees into the jungle.

"I have to find good killing ground. Park says the creature will seek me out. It'll hunt me down. So I'm heading for the plateau and the hills. I need open ground for the beast to cross to get to me."

Moving cautiously through the jungle, Garrick listens intently. The air is rich with scents of plants and wet ground. It is stale and the heat brings perspiration to his temples. Never one to know the names of trees, Garrick notes several types. Easing his way around thick bushes, he has to maneuver around vines and through thick underbrush.

The sensation of moving almost noiselessly through the jungle thrills Garrick. Knowing the great beast could reach out for him at any second keeps his pulse high, keeps his senses alert. The buzzing of insects rises and falls like waves moving to a distant shore.

It is slow but careful progress. When Garrick glances at his watch he sees its been an hour. When he looks again at his watch, another hour is gone. He stops next to a banana tree and slips between its broad leaves. Sitting, he pulls out his canteen and takes a measured drink of water.

He returns the canteen to his belt, wipes sweat from his eyes and slips back out from between the leaves. The ground seems to rise and Garrick moves even more carefully. Rounding a large tree, there is a break in the foliage and he sees the high plateau ahead and the hills beyond.

He smiles to himself, wipes sweat away from his eyes again and pushes forward. Three steps later, the incessant buzz of the insects stops. Garrick freezes. Raising the rifle he looks around carefully. If it's close, he knows he won't have much time to shoot. The trees and bushes are pressed too close.

Garrick waits.

The insect noise does not return.

He can hear his heartbeat now, thundering in his ears.

He swallows dryly and goes down on his haunches and listens and watches.

His hands begin to shake and Garrick feels a numbing fear.

My God, he thinks. *What if I freeze?*

A twig snaps to his right and he wields the rifle around just as the Ponerine rushes forward, its ice-tong jaws open wide.

"Aw!" Garrick raises the rifle and fires at the enormous head. The bullet ricochets off. The huge creature is hideous, its thorny skin deeply pitted and hairy.

He fires again and then leaps away from the snapping jaws. He stumbles to a large tree, gets his footing and runs headlong through the jungle. Running zig-zag, he is too frightened to look back. He runs as hard as he can, runs wildly through a jungle that clings to his every movement.

A crash behind him pushes him faster and Garrick races, legs pumping, rifle held out front to push away the foliage. The ground suddenly falls away and Garrick tumbles down a cut-back and slides into a small stream. Rising, he runs headlong down the stream.

His recovers his footing and uses the narrow area next to the stream to increase his speed. The thick canopy of the jungle overhead draws him into a semi-darkness. Garrick runs until the oxygen-starved leg muscles cramp, until his heaving lungs convulse and he cannot do anything but fall.

Garrick manages to crawl to a tree, turn himself around and raise the rifle. Wrenching, he gasps for air, his eyes wet with perspiration. His arms are so weak he can barely hold the rifle.

It takes a long time for the pain to ease.

Garrick wipes his eyes again and again. They register a dizzying world of dark greens and frightening grays. He struggles to focus. Long moments later, he hears something. It is the ocean, it is the sea, bubbling to shore. No, it is a monsoon, a wild rush of water that will sweep him away. He closes his eyes as he continues gasping for air.

The stabbing in his lungs finally eases and he realizes it's not the ocean, not the sea, not a wild rush of water. It's the stream. And, as the noise of his own breathing decreases in his ears, he hears – insects.

He wants to ask how? How did I get away? He wants to put it on the recorder, only his mouth can't form the words yet. Slowly, Garrick lets the rifle down, cradling it in his lap.

And eventually, Garrick can speak.

"I don't know how. But I got away. I'm next to a stream now. Maybe the water masked my scent. I don't know."

And he realizes something that makes his stomach turn sour.

"Why didn't I research the damn ant last night? I don't believe I've come to this hunt with no working knowledge of my quarry. How could I have been so dumb?"

Garrick knows the answer but won't say it.

It's an insect, a lower form of life, so low he never thought much about them. Ever.

Eventually Garrick can move. Eventually he crawls to the stream, leans forward and tastes the sweet water of the gurgling stream. Eventually he can stand and move.

It isn't until he's walking again, rifle held in front of him, that he realizes something and whispers into the recorder. "My 30-06 did not penetrate the ant's hide."

Impossible.

Must have been a glancing blow.

Suddenly, the canopy above opens and the bright light causes Garrick to shield his eyes. The wide, grassy plateau lies in front of him and the green hills beyond.

Slipping behind the last tree before the plateau, Garrick gathers himself. He reloads the Browning and checks his gear. "If the ant catches me out on the plateau, it's over.

"Maybe," he whispers, "I'll wait until night." And it occurs to him again and he curses himself. "Damn Ponerine may be a better night hunter."

Sitting, he goes over his options.

"I have night goggles. I could wait and try at night. I could hide in the grass if it comes. I'll be able to see it at least. I can rest here and eat and get stronger."

And he convinces himself, settles back against the tree trunk and breaks out the cold rations he'd brought along, including the mega-vitamins. He brushes the leaves and twigs from his beard before he eats. After, he slips back into the jungle and re-fills his canteen before returning to his tree sanctuary.

As the slow, steamy hours creep by, Garrick watches the jungle, listens to it, becomes part of it. He focuses all of his senses and waits. Eventually, his eye-lids become heavy. He closes them for a moment, listening carefully for any sound. Eventually, the steady hum of the insects makes him more tired and he closes his eyes for long seconds at a time.

His mind drifts.

He feels himself drifting.

And dreams –

He sees animals running, fawn colored animals in a dust storm, racing across an African veldt.

Then his father's face beams at Garrick from across a campfire. His grandfather is there too and both men are bragging about the great hunts they'd experienced. Garrick is eleven. His father suddenly asks something about Garrick running away from an ant. His grandfather laughs. Garrick tells them it was hideous. It was enormous. But they don't understand. He can't make them understand the Ponerine's size.

He sees his mother now, sitting next to him. Her warm brown eyes look at Garrick and she understands, but says nothing. It makes him feel better, not because she understands, but because she's young again and is so pretty sitting next to him. She grabs his hand with her strong hand and squeezes.

Then Garrick sees his ex-wife's face, close to his. Angry, she snarls at him as she picks up his hunting gear and throws it into the fire.

"You ran away from an ant!" She screeches and Garrick's father and grandfather laugh. Garrick wants to hit his ex so badly, but he remembers and tells her they are divorced and she has no business in his life. And she fades. And the other faces fade.

Garrick opens his eyes and it's dark. He quickly dons the night-vision goggles and checks his watch. Park had explained how he allowed the natural cycle of night to envelope the land. He makes a mental note of the time. It will become night again at the same time tomorrow. If Park is anything, he is meticulous. Unlike the ant, Garrick now knows when darkness will come. It might help. Anything he learns might help, he tells himself.

And slowly, cautiously, he moves away from the jungle on to the plain.

Without stars, without moonlight, the darkness is so complete, he has to tune the night-vision goggles to its maximum intensity before he can distinguish the plain in front of him.

Garrick moves steadily across it, directly for the dark hills.

As the hours pass and his legs burn from the constant strain, Garrick sees the hills as darker-than-black in front of him. He presses on, scanning the terrain around him and behind him with the night-vision.

And finally, he reaches the base of the hills.

And he starts climbing.

And he maneuvers around boulders and scrub brush.

And he presses on.

Until – in a blinding rush, the day returns.

Garrick pulls off the goggles as he falls to the hard ground. He presses his fingers against his eyes and then covers them with the palms of his hands.

"Damn," he growls into the recorder. "Park just flips on a switch. No dawn!"

A half hour later, Garrick checks his watch again, registering the time the light came back on. Rising, he finds a crease between two hills. He sees a cave in the crease and moves to check it out.

"It's perfect," he tells himself a half hour later as he gathers firewood outside the cave.

An hour after this, he's sitting behind a small, flat boulder outside the cave. Scanning the plateau and the narrow passage between the hills that leads up to the cave, he tells the recorder, "I've found a perfect killing zone."

Garrick rests the Browning atop the flat boulder. He pulls the ammo bandoleer off and places it next to the rifle, then mounts the telescopic sight to the top of the Browning. Pulling out his binoculars, he scans the plateau. Nothing.

So he lights a fire, pulls out a tin of beef and opens it. The tin unfolds into a small pan and he cooks the beef over the open fire. Sizzling, the smell of cooking meat makes Garrick's stomach rumble.

"I must ration my water carefully. I haven't found a stream in the hills yet. Fortunately, the cave I've chosen has a rear exit small enough for me to squeeze through, in case of emergency."

He looks back at the cave entrance. Seven feet in diameter, there's no way the Ponerine can get inside.

Garrick pulls off his belt and checks the emergency beacon Park gave him just prior to miniaturization. The red light still flashes every six seconds on the top of the beacon. He runs his fingers over the emergency extraction button, but doesn't push it.

How had Park explained it? Push the button and the sensors above would locate Garrick. Park would let down a rescue pod. "Climb into it," Park said, "And I'll hoist you away."

"After I kill the beast," Garrick says to his recorder, "I'll just waltz back to the chair in the clearing and push the routine extraction button. No emergency here."

The beef tastes wonderful and revives Garrick. After eating he checks the plateau with his binoculars and scans the distant jungle for the beast, but sees nothing. Lying on the ground next to the boulder, he sets his watch alarm to ring in an hour and drifts off the sleep.

The alarm goes off and Garrick rises and checks the kill zone. Nothing. He re-sets the alarm and drifts back to sleep.

The fourth time the alarm goes off, Garrick sits up and there it is. More than half-way across the plateau, its head lowered, its antennae waving over the ground where Garrick had walked. The Ponerine heads directly for him.

Calming himself, Garrick carefully puts away the binoculars and lifts the Browning. He sets its sights on the Ponerine. The scope's cross-hairs aimed at the front of the ant's head, Garrick squeezes off a round. The rifle kicks and Garrick sees a slight puff of dust rise from the ant's head. The ant does not react.

Garrick re-sights the Browning and fires again. Again the bullet strikes the ant's exoskeleton and again bounces away. Garrick aims at the crease between the ant's head and body and fires. Nothing. He shoots at a leg, misses, then shoots again and the bullet strikes, but bounces off.

Frustrated, Garrick aims for the right antennae. He shoots and shoots again. He reloads the Browning and continues firing. The ant does not slow down, does not change its path, does not even look up to see where the objects striking it comes from. It just keeps coming.

Garrick concentrates his fire at the base of the right antennae. He shoots at it again and again, seeing his bullets strike with no effect. He wipes sweat from his brow and wipes his sweaty hands on his shirt and continues firing.

The Ponerine moves directly for him and reaches the base of the hill where it stops and runs its antennae over the low rocks. Garrick fires again and the bullet strikes the antennae again.

"It's like shooting an armored military vehicle."

The Ponerine lifts its head and twists it to one side. Garrick quickly aims at the exposed eye and fires. The ant's head flinches this time. It lifts its front legs. Garrick fires again at the eye. The ant shakes its enormous head, bows forward and starts up the low rise in the crease between the hills, directly for Garrick.

Dripping sweat and breathing hard, Garrick continues firing at the right antennae as the ant moves inexorably for him.

"It's taking its time."

Garrick fires again, the butt of the rifle slamming against his cheek this time.

Standing, he rubs his cheek and watches the ant slowly approach. Leaving the Browning to cool-off on the boulder, he picks up his belt, the ammo bandoleer and canteen and walks back into the cave.

Gathering some of the firewood he'd collected outside, Garrick piles the firewood within a round circle of stones just inside the cave's entrance. He puts his belt back on, pulls the red, fire accelerant flask from the belt and pours accelerant on the wood.

"Every beast on Octavion *and* Earth is afraid of fire," he tells the recorder, reassuringly.

Garrick steps out of the cave and falls back immediately. The Ponerine, moving at breakneck speed, is there, jaws snapping as it bolts for Garrick. Scrambling over the flat boulder, the ant steps on the Browning and sends it sailing.

Garrick lunges back into the cave, takes out a lighter and lights the firewood. It roars to life and he backs away.

"How in hell did it get up here so fast? It wasn't half-way up the hill!"

Garrick withdraws his Bowie knife and backs deeper into the cave. The ground shudders and a loud scraping sound brushes against the cave's entrance. The ant presses its jaws forward, the ice-tongs reach into the cave. Garrick falls down and crawls back on all fours.

His hand shakes so hard he drops the knife. He picks it up quickly.

"What do I do? What do I *do*?"

Smoke floats his way and he wonders if the damn ant has blocked the entrance. He coughs.

"Dammit!" Garrick pulls off his shirt, steps forward and fans the smoke toward the ant. Stepping to his right, he sees the entrance is clear, so he fans his shirt again and pushes the smoke out of the cave.

Soon the fire dies down to a steady flame. Garrick quits fanning and inches forward. He peeks through the opening and sees the ant's antennae waving from just beyond the rise where he fired at it.

"Great!"

Falling back, Garrick sits behind the fire and curses himself. "Damn, I knew I should have brought a back-up weapon." He thinks about the large bore revolver he inherited from his father and realizes what good would it do against the giant beast.

"I'm sitting here now. Calming myself. At this point the Ponerine has the strategic advantage. But I have my brain and a human brain can think of a way to kill anything."

Garrick leans back on his hands and watches the antennae outside. His arms begin to shiver so he has to sit up. He's sure of something he won't tell the recorder. He's sure he's never been this frightened in his life.

Stoking the fire with the tip of the knife, Garrick looks back at the pile of firewood. "I have enough wood to last a while."

When he looks back out of the cave, the antennae are gone. Waiting, he catches a whiff of a sour, acidic scent.

"Is that the ant? Does it smell like that?" He doesn't say it, but shakes his head, knowing he should have read up on the creature.

Looking around again he notices how several of the pieces of firewood are long and straight. He pulls three forward and starts sharpening their ends with the Bowie knife. It is sweaty work and Garrick paces himself.

Keeping a wary watch outside the cave, Garrick creates three fire-hardened spears, putting each tip in the fire and rubbing them out on the rocks next to the fire. He places the spears on the floor behind him, stands and stretches. With his Bowie knife in hand, he creeps forward and peeks out of the cave. The ant is nowhere to be seen. He looks for the Browning but can't see it either.

"It's probably laying in wait, just beyond the rise."

Garrick takes a cautious step forward, then remembers how fast the Ponerine moved and steps back. Moving around the fire again, he places more wood in it, then catches a stronger whiff of the acid smell. It wafts over him as he watches the flames and slowly, he realizes the flames are flickering toward the front of the cave and the smell comes from the cave's rear. He turns quickly, wielding the Bowie knife.

"Wait. The rear entrance is too small. I can barely squeeze through it."

Another breath of sweet acid scent flows across Garrick. Rising, he pulls a burning log from the fire and moves slowly toward the cave's rear. He holds the log high like a torch and squeezes the smooth handle of the Bowie knife. Stepping carefully, Garrick takes the long turn to the left. He stops after completing the turn and peers ahead.

"Where's the opening?"

His throat suddenly dry, he feels the hair standing on his arms. His knees feel weak when he takes another step forward. Holding the torch and Bowie knife in front, Garrick inches along the narrow cave.

He sees a faint light ahead and moves for it. He hears a rock fall and the faint light disappears. It takes several minutes, but he finds the rear entrance, which is now blocked by boulders. And as he stands next to it, he hears a faint scraping sound from above. No – from the side. No, it comes from beyond the boulders.

"It's sealed up the rear exit," Garrick falls back on unsteady legs.

Backing through the cave, it isn't until he reaches the fire that he realizes.

"If it's back there around the other side of the hill, I can get the Browning."

Dropping the log back on the fire, Garrick wipes his sweaty hands on his pants, and grips the Bowie knife with both hands. He moves forward and peeks out the cave. Looking around carefully, he creeps forward, sniffing the air. The flat boulder is only a few feet away. It takes a full minute to find the Browning and he feels a well of excitement in his chest as he reaches for it. Lifting it, a sinking feeling comes to his stomach. The barrel is bent at a forty-five degree angle.

Garrick hears a scraping sound to his right, drops the Browning and runs headlong back for the cave, diving in over the fire and tumbling in the dirt. Sitting up and baring the knife, he looks back and sees nothing. He pulls out his canteen and takes a long drink. His hand shake so, he spills precious water on his chest. He puts the canteen down and closes his eyes.

"I have to think!"

He smells it before he hears the loud scraping sound at the front of the cave. In amazement, Garrick watches the ant use its jaws to scrape open the cave's entrance.

Garrick stands and backs away, his heart stammering, his knees quivering. He raises his knife, then lowers it as the ant's ice-tongs scrape away the rocks.

"It's working it's way into the cave. Breaking the rocks with its jaws."

Garrick picks up a spear and stokes the fire. "When its face comes into view I'll gouge its eyes out."

Surprised at the confidence in his voice, Garrick grabs his canteen and takes another drink. Then he sits and watches the ant's slow progress and feels detached from the scene, as if he's watching it from the comfort of his living room, instead of the dead-end cave.

Eventually the cave's opening is large enough for half of the ant's head to be seen clearly. Close-up, it's so alien. Garrick is riveted. Dark brown in color, the exoskeleton is rough and deeply pitted. Horny, it is fierce looking and hideous with uneven strands of black hair that remind Garrick of a cat's whiskers.

The acidic scent grows and Garrick backs away. Pulling back also, the ant moves an eye to the opening and looks in at Garrick. The compound eyes is cold and black and lifeless. Rising quickly, Garrick grabs a log and starts to throw it at the eye when he notices something that causes him to freeze.

A line of yellowish-green liquid drips from the corner of the eye. It oozes from a gouge in the eye and Garrick knows the Browning did strike true.

Stepping forward, he throws the burning log at the eye. It strikes just above the gouge and bounces off. The ant takes a step back, then another, its antennae tapping against the cave's entrance.

Garrick sees another streak of yellow-green ooze at the base of the right antennae. The antennae is bent slightly and does not swing around as controlled as the other antennae.

"So. You're not indestructible, are you?"

Pausing a moment. The ant moves forward, its jaws chipping the rock again.

"All right!" Garrick picks up more wood and puts it in the fire. Then he sits and pulls his three fire-hardened spears and puts their tips in the flames.

He withdraws the black, cyanide flask and lies it next to the fire. With trembling hands, Garrick reaches for his canteen, opens it and hesitates a moment. He presses his lips to the spout and drinks down the last of his water.

He puts the canteen back in its pouch on his belt and wipes sweat from his face and hands. The close confines of the cave is stifling. Garrick struggles to get his eyes to focus on the ant.

He watches as the creature slowly and inexorably widens the cave's entrance. When the spear tips glow red, he pulls them out of the fire and rubs them on the rocks, sharpening them until they are no longer hot. And he waits.

"The acid smell is so intense, my eyes burn." Garrick closes his eyes and then blinks his eyelids to bring tears to wash away the heat.

"I have to act now."

Garrick opens the cyanide flask carefully. His hand trembles as he pours the colorless liquid on the tip of the first spear. He closes the flask and leaves it away from the fire. Standing, Garrick points the spear at the huge, compound eye peering in at him. The Ponerine's jaw scrapes the rock again, sending a chill through Garrick.

"Now!" Garrick yells as he lunges forward, racing past the fire, shoving the spear tip at the eye. The collision causes Garrick to stumble and fall against the cave's side.

A deafening roar reverberates through the cave and the ant pulls back, the spear stuck near the corner of its right eye. Garrick lifts himself as the ant swings its head around and the spear falls away. The ant roars again and Garrick looks closely. The sound doesn't come from the ant's mouth, but Garrick cannot see where it comes from as the ant's antennae swing back toward him and the beast comes forward again.

The ice-tong jaws snap loudly.

The ant continues its excavation.

Garrick retreats and grabs the second spear. He pours a larger amount of the hydrocyanic acid on the tip.

Hoisting the spear, Garrick takes in a deep breath and charges the ant again, aiming for the same peering right eye. The ant flinches just as the spear strikes and Garrick slams to the ground face first, the hideous jaw snapping over his head.

Garrick crawls back and doesn't realize he's screaming until he's well behind the fire.

He grabs the final spear and struggles to catch is breath. The superheated air is almost unbreatheable now. And the ant continues its meticulous work. Garrick waits for the strength to return to his arms and legs.

The jaws work against the rock and the eye keeps peering in at Garrick. And he sees the bright yellow-green streak is wider along the bottom of the ant's eye and feels a faint hope.

"It's wounded."

But the wound seems to have no effect on the creature.

Garrick pours the rest of the hydrocyanic acid on his last spear tip.

"I'm charging it again. There's enough cyanide on this spear to kill a dozen tyrannosaurs." Garrick's voice is scratchy.

He swallows bitter saliva, raises his last spear and rushes for the eye. He aims for the yellow swatch and lunges, bracing himself for the collision. The spear strikes the eye and Garrick slips forward and hangs on to the spear.

An ear-splitting roar washes over Garrick. Slipping, he regains his footing and pushes the spear forward. It slides into the eye and the ant jerks back. Garrick hangs on and is lifted.

The jaws snap shut just below Garrick's feet and he pulls them up. The ant swings its head and Garrick holds on. And then a bright light blinds Garrick and it takes a full second to realize he's outside the cave, hanging on to the spear as the ant raises its head and the spear sinks further into the eye.

The ant's head swings to the right and Garrick crashes into a boulder. Reaching up with his left hand, he pulls himself up on the boulder and lets go of the spear. The ant staggers and swings its head from side to side. When the spear moves back toward Garrick, he grabs it and shoves it deeper into the ant's eye.

The jaws snap against the boulder.

Garrick feels himself rise again and waiver in the air for a long second before the ant's front legs buckle. Garrick presses his weight against the spear as it sinks further into the eye.

And slowly, the ant's head falls forward, bringing Garrick to the ground. Jumping back, Garrick grabs a rock and smashes it against the end of the spear. He pounds it into the ant's head and hears a cracking. Standing in a flood of yellow-green liquid, Garrick smashes the end of the spear again and again, until he can no longer lift his arms.

He falls back and watches the ant. Its back legs twitch and Garrick moves away and leans against another boulder until his gasping breaths return to normal.

Sometime later, Garrick rises on aching legs and gathers whatever wood he can find. He piles the wood around the ant, keeping away from the ice tong jaws that lie unmoving now. Moving in slow-motion, Garrick gathers enough firewood to completely surround the ant.

The fire in the cave is nearly out, when Garrick goes back in. He digs out the fire accelerant flask from his belt. Moving on wobbly legs, Garrick picks a burning stick out of the fire and goes back outside.

Standing next to the great beast, Garrick struggles to speak, to record his great triumph. But his throat is too dry. He cannot speak. Raising the fire accelerant flask, Garrick splashes the liquid against the ant's side and on the wood. Slowly, he moves around the Ponerine, anointing it with accelerant, blessing it for its ugliness, wetting it for the inevitable fire.

Standing next to the ant's destroyed eye, Garrick pauses and sticks the burning stick into the ground. Withdrawing his Bowie knife, he reaches up and pulls down the ant's antennae. It takes several hacks, but he manages to break away the antennae's tip.

"This is my trophy," he tells the ant in a barely audible voice.

Lifting the burning stick, Garrick blows on it and the flame dances. He steps back and tosses the stick against the ant. The flame quickly engulfs the great beast. And Garrick finds the flat boulder, the one he'd rested the Browning on so long ago, and sits and watches the ant burn.

Sometime later, Garrick's dusty voice says, "I need water."

He forces himself to rise and climb off the boulder. He looks across the plateau toward the green trees and the gurgling stream. He licks his parched lips and tries to swallow, but cannot.

"I'll never make it," he whispers, hoarsely.

Pressing his rear against the boulder, Garrick remembers, and laughs to himself. He reaches for the emergency beacon but it's not on his belt. He looks around and sees it on the ground next to the boulder he'd slammed into. The beacon is in three pieces.

On his knees, Garrick tries to put it back together, but it's no use.

"Dammit!" Garrick throws it into the ant fire in disgust.

Sitting in the dirt, he covers his head with his arms and struggles to think clearly. The words come to him as if in a dream.

"I need rest. Sleep and then I'll have enough strength to cross the plateau. After all, I just killed the most formidable predator in the known universe."

Garrick feels a smile break on his sore face as he rises and slowly makes his way back to the cave. Just as he enters, the light outside disappears. Garrick nods and moves beyond the fire to a flat patch on the floor and goes down on all fours. Lying on his back, Garrick closes his eyes.

And slowly, the floor seems to fall away . . .

The light wakes him in the morning and Garrick rises to an unbearable thirst and a biting hunger. Moving stiffly, he exits the cave and walks around the burnt carcass of his kill. The stench nearly gags him.

Taking a last look at the great beast, Garrick heads down to the plateau and walks in a straight line for the trees in the distance. Reliving the kill, Garrick makes mental notes on how he will explain it to his recorder as soon as he relieves his parched throat.

He plays it over and over again in his mind, the cave and the fire-hardened spears and the sickly yellow-green blood and the death throws of the great beast. He can still feel the heat of its funeral pyre on his face.

His mind drifts to thoughts his grandfather bounding through the Magenta Forest, felling dinosaurs. Garrick's father walks behind the old man, checking off the kills from a checklist. His father, still a boy, beams proudly as he checks off a dead stegosaur.

Garrick sees himself now, standing next to the dead Ponerine. His grandfather and father stop and stare at him and he tells them. *This* is the ant. They stand amazed as they look at the great beast.

Garrick's mother moves from behind them and has the same look on her face she had when they teased him over the fire. And when Garrick thinks about it, his mother always had that gentle, knowing look on her face, even as she lay on her deathbed.

"They're all dead now," he says aloud. "Even the ant."

Garrick walks without looking around, walks straight and true and keeps walking. It isn't until he nearly trips over a root does he realize he's made it to the jungle forest. He listens but cannot hear the stream.

Moving into the woods, he listens intently. Finally he hears it and feels its coolness before he spots it off to his right. Stumbling forward, Garrick dives into the stream and sinks his face into it.

He drinks and the cool water burns and then soothes him as nothing has ever soothed him. And he rolls on his back and lies in the stream, dipping his head to the side to drink again and again.

Like a rejuvenating potion, the water revives Garrick. Sitting in the stream, he pulls out his canteen and fills it. He drinks more water, drinks until his belly can hold no more.

Rising on renewed legs, he moves into the woods for the chair where he'll signal Park to remove him.

"I lost my voice during the struggle," Garrick tells his recorder. "I will recall as much as I can as I move back through the woods to the recovery chair." He recounts the titanic battle, blow by blow. Then he recalls the exploits of his grandfather, stories he'd heard as a child of the good old days when safaris were run across Octavion, when the thud of dead tyrannosaurs and dead brontosaurs echoed. He even recalls the legends of mother Earth and the great white hunters of Africa – his ancestors.

No need to hold them in awe anymore. Garrick knows he's their equal now. Maybe their better. He's slain the great *Ponerine*.

"The thrill cannot be described in words," he says. "The power of death is intoxicating. This has been, for me, the ultimate hunt. Next time, I'll have Park put two ants in the jungle."

Pausing between sentences, Garrick notices the incessant chatter of the insects has stopped.

He freezes, then lets out a laugh.

"It's dead. One Ponerine. One man. And I killed it."

Looking around as he starts forward again, Garrick waits for the insects to start up again. When they don't he stops again. He reaches down and touches his trophy, the piece of Ponerine antenna hanging from his belt.

A thud behind him turns Garrick around just as the ice-tong jaws of a Ponerine snaps against his chest. The excruciating pain is blinding as the ant folds Garrick in two and starts eating him alive.

• • •

Jonas Park pulls his eye away from the magnifying glass and stretches.

"So much for Mr. Jon Garrick."

Park climbs down from the platform suspended next to his terrarium and begins the long process of dismantling his miniaturization machine and packing away his Earth forest of oaks and banana trees and hungry Ponerine warrior ants, and the ghosts of hungry hunters.

Six hours later, Park is in the driver's seat of his oversized truck, heading across the vast Sienna Plateau, smiling as he drives beneath the strong sun, in his unending pursuit of the great white hunters of Octavion.

THE END of "A Frightful Fiend"

THE END
of
Backwash of the Milky Way

•

Note from the Publisher
BIG KISS PRODUCTIONS

If you found a typo or two in the book, please don't hold it against us. We are a small group of volunteers dedicated to presenting quality fiction from writers with genuine talent. We tried to make this book as perfect as possible, but we are human and make mistakes.

BIG KISS PRODUCTIONS and the author are proud to sell this book at as low a cost as possible. Even great fiction should be affordable.

Also by the Author

<u>Novels</u>
Battle Kiss
John Raven Beau
Enamored
Slick Time
Mafia Aphrodite
The Big Show
Crescent City Kills
Blue Orleans
The Big Kiss
Grim Reaper
<u>Short Story Collections</u>
New Orleans Confidential
New Orleans Prime Evil
New Orleans Nocturnal
New Orleans Mysteries
New Orleans Irresistible
Hollow Point & The Mystery of Rochelle Marais
LaStanza: New Orleans Police Stories
<u>Screenplay</u>
Waiting for Alaina
<u>Non-Fiction</u>
A Short Guide to Writing and Selling Fiction
Specific Intent

O'Neil De Noux would like to hear from you. If you liked this book or have ANY comment, email him at
denoux3124@yahoo.com

For more information and other book by O'Neil De Noux go to
http://www.oneildenoux.net

O'NEIL DE NOUX

a crime novel

Enamored

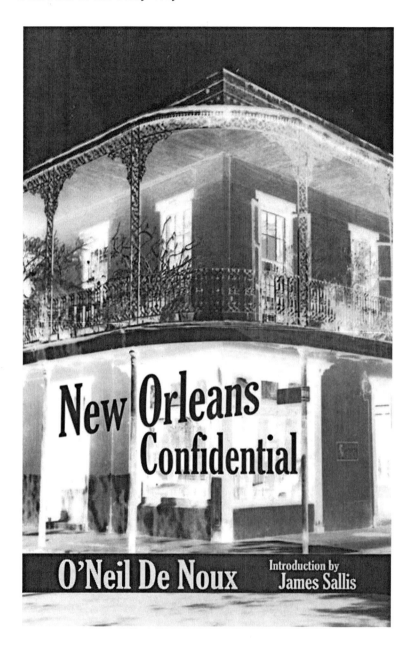

O'Neil De Noux

a sexy caper

Slick Time

CPSIA information can be obtained at www.ICGtesting.com
Printed in the USA
LVOW102145170213

320514LV00002B/37/P